A SPLINTER OF GLASS

Born in Surrey in 1908, John Creasey was the seventh son in a family of nine. For nine years after leaving school he had over twenty different jobs, and then, in 1935, started to make a living from writing. His books have sold over seventy-five million copies and have been translated into twenty-eight different languages. *A Splinter of Glass* is one of the Roger West series, of which there are over fifty titles, many of which have appeared in Pan. John Creasey died in June 1973.

Books by John Creasey in the Ulverscroft Large Print Series:

SEND SUPERINTENDENT WEST
A GUN FOR INSPECTOR WEST
DEATH BY NIGHT
THE PLAGUE OF SILENCE
THE MISTS OF FEAR
THE TERROR TRAP
A SPLINTER OF GLASS
THE LONG SEARCH
THE INFERNO
THE DROUGHT
HANG THE LITTLE MAN

This Large Print Edition
is published by kind permission of
HODDER & STOUGHTON LTD.
London

JOHN CREASEY

A SPLINTER OF GLASS

Complete and Unabridged

ULVERSCROFT
Leicester

First published 1972 by
Hodder & Stoughton Ltd.
London.

First Large Print Edition
published July 1975
SBN 85456 349 0

© John Creasey 1972

Published by
F. A. Thorpe (Publishing) Ltd.
Anstey, Leicestershire
Printed in England

CONTENTS

1	The Splinter	1
2	The Widow	17
3	A Hole in the Ground	31
4	Weakness	44
5	Angela Margerison	60
6	Clue?	74
7	Evidence	90
8	Press Challenge	104
9	Dan Appleby	118
10	Attack	132
11	Motorway	147
12	K & K	162
13	Missing Equipment	178
14	Wanted Man	193
15	Waldmann	207
16	Confrontation	222
17	Youth v. Age	237
18	Flora	253
19	The Arches	269
20	Tentacles	285

ACKNOWLEDGEMENT

I am most grateful to E. S. Pearse, former managing director, J. W. C. Poole, managing director, Laboratory Division of James A. Jobling & Co. Ltd., and D. Curtis, special studies controller, Group Strategy Division, all of whom gave me such invaluable help in the technical details in this book. Any errors which may appear are due not to the slightest misguidance but to author's licence!

JOHN CREASEY

1
THE SPLINTER

DETECTIVE Officer Venables snatched his hand from the floor, and drew in a hissing breath. It echoed strangely about the big, empty room, reaching the hall where two men were talking. Venables, who had been crouching, sprang up like a jack-in-the-box and looked at the puncture in his right forefinger. Blood was already welling up into a tiny globule which grew larger and began to run over the finger and drip on to the floor. He put his finger to his mouth and sucked, and at the same time took a handkerchief from the left-hand pocket of his loose-fitting grey tweed jacket. Doing so, he caught sight of a man standing in the doorway.

Finger in mouth, handkerchief ballooning as he shook it out of its folds, one of the youngest detectives in London's Metropolitan Police Force came face to face with one of its senior and most renowned detectives: Chief Detective Superintendent Roger West.

Venables snatched his hand away, unaware that he smeared blood over his lip and chin.

"Hurt yourself?" demanded West.

"Er — it's nothing, sir. Just a splinter of glass."

"They can be very painful," West said, glancing down at Venables' right hand. The finger was throbbing painfully and the warm blood flowed. "That's more than a splinter," he went on. "Let me have a look."

Reluctantly, Venables did so. He felt a little foolish and also felt chagrined, for this was the first time he had worked on a case with "Handsome" West in charge and he had had dreams of distinguishing himself. There was little chance now! Here was West, holding his wrist and turning the hand palm upwards and then straightening the forefinger by holding it on each side of the nail, as if he had had a lot of practice; as indeed he had, with his children. The blood still welled up.

"Is the water still on here, do you know?" he asked.

"Yes, sir — at all events, the W.C. works."

"Get that finger under the cold-water tap," advised West. "And you'll need an antiseptic and a plaster. Green!" he called.

Another man, who had stayed out of sight, came to the doorway.

"Sir?"

What Green saw became indelibly printed on his mind. West, a six-footer, broad but lean at waist and hips, with hair that looked as flaxen as when he had joined the Force over twenty years ago, holding the hand of the very tall, very thin Venables, whose black hair was so thick and unruly it was almost as if he had given up trying to groom it. Clean-shaven, his skin appearing unusually white by contrast to his hair, he had big eyes and bushy black eyebrows. Where Roger West was good-looking in a film-star way — once his looks had been a very great disadvantage — Venables was a caricature: too tall, too thin, with hands and feet disproportionately large.

"Get the first-aid box from the car and take it along to the kitchen," Roger ordered.

"Really, sir, it's nothing," Venables protested weakly.

"Looks as if you gashed your finger," Green said. "I'll get the box, sir."

He went off. Venables wrapped his handkerchief about the finger, thanking his luck and his mother that it was clean, and moved towards the door. When he reached the doorway he felt a wave of dizziness, and almost staggered. For a moment he could not think clearly, but as the dizziness passed he became acutely conscious of West again, and straightened up. But the effort was too much and he swayed.

West, coming from behind, took his elbow and without a word, led him towards the kitchen. This house followed the pattern of many which had been built between the wars: solidly built, with the front door leading on to a fairly wide hall from which two doors opened, both on the right. A staircase rose straight and steep, and alongside was a passage leading to a doorway, wide open, and a small room and a kitchen beyond. The window of the kitchen was right opposite the door, and showed autumn leaves from fruit trees carpeting a long, narrow garden.

Passage, communicating room and kitchen were all empty. Footsteps of other policemen sounded on the bare boards overhead; West's and Venables' footsteps echoed in the narrower confines down here. The kitchen was fairly large, the sink unit, the only piece of equipment in the room, being in one corner behind the door.

West turned on the cold tap, and water spouted.

"They certainly cleaned this place up," he remarked.

"Looks like a professional job," Venables said. He still felt foolish and disconsolate, now that the dizzy spell had passed, he could not understand what had come over him. West adjusted the tap so that water flowed at a gentle pace, and then, holding Venables' wrist, place the finger under the tap. Blood had flowed up into the crook of the fingers and spread along all the lines, making palm and fingers look like a map etched in bright red. With his other hand, West pushed back the cuff of Venables' jacket sleeve; there was a button off the shirt cuff, so that went up too.

Suddenly Venables gave a nervous little laugh.

5

"What's funny?" asked West, mildly.

"This reminds me of a time when I was a kid, and cut my finger," Venables said. "My father did exactly the same as you have, and there was a button off *that* shirt cuff, too."

"My wife used to spend her life sewing on buttons and mending tears. How does that feel?"

"It stings a bit, sir, but it's nothing to worry about, really."

Roger West peered more closely at the finger, washed nearly clean of blood and revealing a small but obviously deep gash; a typical cut from broken glass. It looked clean enough. He placed his thumbs on either side of the cut, and pressed slightly, opening it; blood flowed again. He let it close and then pressed on top of the cut itself.

"Hurt?"

"Not to say hurt, sir."

"It would if there was any glass left in," Roger said. He heard Green coming along the passage, carrying a small first-aid box which was standard equipment for all police cars in the Metropolitan area, and a roll of paper-towelling. He stood aside, so that

Green could take over, and asked almost as an afterthought: "What did you mean by a 'professional job', Venables?"

Venables thought: so he knows my name.

"The way it was cleaned out, sir — hardly a speck of dust and the woodwork seemed polished."

"How did you get that splinter?"

"Well, sir," said Venables, while Green was dabbing an antiseptic-soaked cotton-wool ball on the cut, "I wasn't sure whether the floor had been wax polished or whether it had been treated with Perma-Pol, that stuff which just has to be swept or vacuumed and lasts for years."

"What was it, in fact?" asked West.

"Wax, sir. I was scraping some off with my fingernail."

"More fool you," declared Green.

That remark, reflected Roger, explained why burly Green, at thirty-nine, would never be more than a detective sergeant, whereas Venables, who couldn't be much more than twenty-five, would probably become an inspector in a comparatively short time. These days, promotion came quickly to a good man, and forty was a fairly common retiring age. There was no point in saying that this was a useful piece of investigation; no point in ruffling Green.

"Any idea how long it had been done?" asked Roger.

"Fairly recently, sir. I'd already tried one spot and sniffed: the smell of the polish was fairly strong. Hadn't hung about the room much, though. The windows must have been left open for some time, unless whoever did it used an air-freshening spray." Venables' words were in no way boastful or self-righteous; he was very matter-of-fact about the whole thing, taking it for granted that observing and checking such things was his job. "Do we know how long the house has been empty, sir?"

"Six days," answered Roger, "according to local information gathered from several sources."

"I thought it was seven — sir," Green intervened. He seemed a little put out, possibly because Venables' information was being taken so seriously. "I think this will be all right now, if I put a plaster on fairly tightly."

"Nice work," Roger approved.

"Sir," said Venables.

"Yes?"

"May I know what we're looking for?" Venables tried to repress his eagerness but did not succeed.

"You mean you haven't been told?"

"Er — not specifically," Venables said. "I — er — I was just told to look for anything left behind by the previous occupiers, and any marks on the floor, walls and paintwork. There are very few, sir — everything has been so thoroughly cleaned. That's why I thought it must be a professional job, sir. The paintwork has been washed with a strong detergent, so have the walls, which have a washable paint or distemper covering."

Roger West remarked: "A really professional job, then. Yes: you may know why we're in this house, but keep it to yourself, we don't want a leakage to the newspapers. We have a pretty strong clue that some of the bullion from the London docks was brought here."

"Bullion!" exclaimed Venables.

"Gold bars," explained Green, as if to a child.

"Why, over a half million pounds' worth was hi-jacked!" Venables gasped.

"That's right," Roger agreed.

"It must have been over six months ago, surely."

"Eight," volunteered Green, as he finished placing the plaster into position. "That should be all right."

"Thanks." Venables pressed the injured finger gingerly. "Seems fine."

"Sergeant," Roger said to Green, "go and see how things are getting on upstairs. And then take one officer and start checking the neighbours. We need to know if there have been many movements of vans or trucks noticed about the time the tenants left. We may have to make it a full-scale check but see what information you get first."

"Right, sir." Green went off with the first-aid box, and soon they heard him clumping up the uncarpeted stairs.

"Gosh!" exclaimed Venables, boyishly. "You mean that the place may have been cleaned up to make sure there were no traces of gold left? Tell you what there *is*, sir — in this little in-between room." The gangling man actually started for the "in-between" room first, then stood aside for Roger to go ahead. This room had only a small window of frosted glass, so was very dark. There was a door leading to a kind of alleyway outside, and Venables pushed past Roger to open this; chill air and bright daylight swept in. "See, sir?" He pointed to the floor alongside the wall which divided the room from the kitchen.

This was a tile-covered floor, sealed at the skirting boards, as washrooms sometimes were. Some patches showed at one side, where a machine — or something heavy — had been stuck to the tiles; after the machine had been removed the adhesive had been scraped and sanded off; with the door closed, these marks had not shown up.

"Something pretty heavy stood there," remarked Venables. "See how the cement between the tiles is cracked?"

"Yes. What would you say it was?" asked West.

"Well, sir, if I didn't know the association I might have said a big boiler, there's been a flue here at one time or another." He pointed to a sealed hole in the ceiling. "But too long ago to have been used recently. At a guess, I'd say a lathe — something you could turn the gold bars on, sir, and make shavings. Much easier to melt shavings down than the bars or ingots, and they could then make small bars which would be quite easy to carry and distribute." When West looked at him very straightly but didn't comment, Venables went on anxiously; "Don't you think so, sir?"

"It's quite possible," Roger conceded. "We need some of those tiles up, to see if any gold filings worked their way underneath."

"Good idea, sir," approved Venables happily. "Did you see that film *Paint Your Wagon*, by any chance? Quite good, in a way — there was a gang which tunnelled under the floorboards of bars and saloons where gold dust was used as cash, to filch all the dust which slipped between the cracks."

"I don't think we need to do any tunnelling," Roger said drily. "But we certainly need some of these tiles up. And the skirting boards need checking. My car's outside. Go and tell *Information* on the radio that we need tools to get the job done. And it's urgent," he added, almost grimly.

"I'll tell them, sir!" Venables went off eagerly, holding his right hand chest-high, as if to prevent it from throbbing.

Roger followed the young man thoughtfully. Venables was very bright and unselfconscious and with luck and the right experience, would become a very good detective indeed. His appearance, although against him at first sight, didn't really matter at all. He walked very lightly, in spite of his big feet, and all of his movements were supple, not clumsy in the way of many tall men.

Roger turned into the front room where Venables had caught his hand on the splinter of glass. Little spots of blood, now coagulated to chocolate-brown, indicated the position. Roger went down on one knee, to examine the boards and to look for the splinter. At first he didn't see it, and almost automatically he began to draw his finger along the polished surface, but suddenly he snatched it away: this was how Venables had cut himself. He couldn't see the splinter, which was odd. Then, so was the whole place. He didn't have very much doubt that the gold had been stored here, and that his clue had come too late.

That wasn't surprising, since it had come from a dead man: a note caught in the lining of a wallet, giving the address: *17*,

Lyon Avenue, Chiswick, London, W.4. It was a long and peculiar story. For the dead man, David Margerison, was the only one who had been positively identified after the lorry-load of gold had been hi-jacked from the London docks in as brazen a way as any crime committed in the past ten years. The call for Margerison, who had been recognised by one of the Port of London Authority policemen in charge of security inside the docks, had gone out at once. Not only all the police in Britain but Interpol had been asked to keep a lookout for him. There had been the usual crop of mistaken identities and no real clue about Margerison's whereabouts until his body had been found, floating just beneath the surface of the Thames at Hammersmith — very close to Lyon Avenue. It had been hauled out of the water at half past nine; by half past ten, Roger had been told of the note in his wallet; by eleven o'clock, police from the Yard had arrived here.

It would have been difficult to work more quickly.

Studying the floorboards he suddenly got up, went to his case which Green had left in the hall, unlocked it and took out a magnifying glass with a finger-long handle, fitted with a tiny battery and light. He went back to the spot and used the glass, focussing it until he could see tiny cracks in wood and polish which he hadn't noticed before.

Ah! There was the splinter.

It had lodged nearly parallel with the boards, either entering where one had been split, or else splitting it, and a trick of light from the window concealed it from most angles. There was no sign of blood on it but there was a spot of blood very close. He took out a penknife and began to pry and probe, gradually loosening the splinter. As he worked it away from the wood, he saw how large it was — about an inch long and point-narrow at one end, flat at the other, which was about as wide as a stick from a book of matches and jagged at the edge Venables had caught with his finger. Along one side there was a line of blue, which might prove very useful for identification. Once it was free, he drew a small envelope from his pocket and scooped the splinter in.

And he wondered what, if anything, it could tell him.

As the thought passed through his mind, he saw a small car draw into the kerb, stopping just behind his own car. A woman sat at the wheel. She was dark-haired, and his glimpse of her profile suggested she was both young and attractive. He moved across the room, standing on one side so that he could see her without himself being noticed.

She was undoubtedly most attractive.

A flurry of long, slim legs; a graceful movement as she got out and stood by the side of the car; then her expression seemed to freeze as she stared at the front door. Roger had seldom seen a greater look of alarm.

He wasn't really surprised at her appearance, for he had seen her twice in the past two weeks. She was Angela Margerison, the dead man's wife.

2

THE WIDOW

ROGER did not move from his position.

The woman, still frozen, began to move slowly back towards the car. A policeman, who had been on duty at the porch and must have gone inside the hall for some reason, appeared suddenly; obviously it was the sight of him which had affected Angela Margerison. The policeman's voice sounded, pleasantly enough.

"Can I help you, miss?"

"Er — no. No thank you." Her voice was shrill, as if edged with fear. "I've come to the wrong house." She turned hastily and stretched out her hand to open the car door. Roger walked swiftly across the room and into the hall. The constable, quite young, moved nearer to her.

"Are you sure you're all right, miss?"

"Yes," she said breathlessly. "I — I thought someone I knew lived here, it *must* be the wrong house."

"May I know the name?"

She didn't answer this time but scrambled into the car and slammed the door. She looked terrified. The policeman moved forward very quickly, calling: "Just a moment, miss." But the car engine raced, and the girl slammed it into gear without glancing at him.

He did exactly what Roger hoped he would: grabbed the handle and opened the door. His voice sounded almost absurdly quiet when he repeated: "Just a moment, miss."

She shot the car forward, and the movement jerked the handle out of the policeman's grasp. The door itself swung wildly. She spun the wheel to pass the police car, and for a moment it looked as if the door was bound to slam into the other, but it missed by a fraction of an inch. The constable, his arm badly wrenched, reeled back into the garden wall, and the engine roared.

Roger raced to the front of the police car.

Two or three people were in the street, watching aghast; and Green and another man were in the doorway of the house next door, looking petrified. To them, to everyone in sight it looked as if Roger was going to run straight into the side of the little car, now only a foot away from him.

"*Stop!*" he roared. "*Stop!*"

The girl gave him a glance of sheer terror. The car was now going too fast for him to reach the swaying door. The wheels swung away from him, as the girl leaned sideways to grab the door as it swung close. Her eyes looked huge; her lips were set, showing her teeth. The door slammed. Green and another man raced up, but there was now no chance of catching up with the Mini, which spun left round the corner and out of sight.

"You — you all right, sir?" a man gasped. It was Green.

Roger muttered: "Yes. Drive after her and put a call out for the car as you go." He saw Green now at his best, for the man's reflexes were quite remarkable and he was at the wheel of the black Rover and on the move as quickly as the girl had been; and as it moved off, Roger saw him stretching out for the radio-phone tuned in to *Information* at the Yard.

The policeman was now standing upright, while an elderly woman, obviously anxious, leaned towards him.

"Are you all right?" she demanded. "Are you hurt?"

"No — no, ma'am." The constable straightened up as Roger approached. He looked shaken and dishevelled, his helmet, on one side, giving him the look of a musical comedy policeman. "I'm sorry I let her go, sir."

"She was pretty slick," Roger said. "We'll get her eventually though."

"What on earth —" began the woman, and then she stopped, looking from one to the other in astonishment. "Is she wanted — by the police?"

"You could say that," said Roger, smiling to reassure her. "Do you live in Lyon Avenue?"

"Oh, no. I live in Laurel Avenue, it's two streets along," the woman answered. "I was just passing, that's all. I was only passing." She was middle-aged, red-faced, carrying a packed shopping basket. "I must hurry, I'll be late for my son, he'll be home for his lunch by now." She turned and began to walk away very quickly.

Roger said: "Are you really all right, Constable?"

"Oh, yes, sir!"

"Good." Roger went towards the house, and then out of the corner of his eye saw the uniformed man's right hand, with a smear of blood on it. The blood was almost exactly at the same place as Venables'. "Better go inside and wash that," Roger said gruffly, and went ahead; hesitantly, the man followed him.

Venables was in the hall.

"It's coming, sir," he said eagerly.

"What's coming?"

"The tool-kit — for prising the floor-boards up."

"Oh, of course." How easy it was to forget when under pressure. "All right, do a bit of first-aid in turn, will you, until it comes." He went upstairs where men who had rushed to the windows were now getting back to the job of searching. One plain-clothes man came to the head of the stairs to meet Roger.

"Hallo, Smith," Roger said. "Found anything?"

"Not a thing, sir. The place is as clean as a new pin."

"It's the same downstairs," Roger told him, "but there's an indication that a lathe may have been stuck down on the floor of one of the rooms. Venables has sent for tools. Go and help get some tiles up, will you?"

"Right away, sir."

Roger nodded as he passed, and then went into each of four bedrooms, a bathroom and a W.C. Two more detectives were examining the rooms, which were all absolutely spotless. Roger went to a back window and looked out over the long narrow garden. It was well kept, with a lawn on one side, a crazy paving path in the middle, a flower bed already dug over for winter planting.

A man was behind him.

"Neat-looking place, sir, isn't it?"

"Someone was proud of his garden," Roger said. "Anyone been out there yet?"

"I think Detective Venables has, sir."

"Oh. Thanks." Roger looked right and left, to the houses in the street opposite, their backs all facing this way. There was ugliness and yet symmetry in the red-brick buildings, the grey slate roofs, the identical outbuildings, attached to the houses. Most of the gardens were well cared for, but none better than this.

He recalled his interview with the house agent, round the corner in the High Street.

"Mr. Denton moved in on Monday 1st, sir. There's no doubt about the date. He paid in cash, and took possession before the papers were through. But money makes the mare to go!" The house agent, almost startlingly old and skinny, had given a sudden, rollicking laugh.

The great robbery had taken place on March 10th, about seven months ago. It had probably been planned weeks earlier and, always provided this was the house used by the thieves, this place had been made ready. And whoever had been here had loved gardening.

He drew in his breath, making a sharp hissing sound, swung round and called downstairs.

"Smith! Are you there?"

"Sir!" called Smith, from the passage by the side of the stairs.

"How much have our chaps done in the garden?"

"Practically nothing, sir. Venables was out there for a few minutes, that's all."

"Where is Venables?"

"Here, sir," the lanky young man called.

"I want you to show me what you did in the garden," Roger ordered, and hurried down the stairs. As he reached the foot, the Rover pulled up alongside and next to Green, Roger saw a scared-looking Angela Margerison: so that chase hadn't lasted long, and Green had fully justified himself as a man of action. Venables now appeared in the passage alongside him, his expression one of great eagerness. Roger said: "I won't be a minute," and strode towards the door, reaching the little porch as the woman came round from the far side of the car.

Woman! She wasn't much more than a girl. When he had seen her before, Roger had realised that; been convinced, too, that she had not known that her husband had been involved in the big robbery. Yet her flight made him wonder. Would she have come here except to visit her husband?

He felt a deep sense of disquiet.

He had been in charge of the investigation since the night that the news had broken. He was responsible for all that had happened, including allowing Angela Margerison to go unwatched. It now looked as if that had been a mistake. The way her car had first drawn up outside the house indicated a certain familiarity, as if she had visited it often before.

Now, ahead of Green, who looked enormous behind her, Angela came towards him. Fear still put a bright sheen in her eyes. She *was* tiny, but with a trim figure; her legs and ankles were magnets to a man's eyes; so was her bosom. She wore a black suit with a frilly white blouse and frilly cuffs. He felt that he had known her for a long time.

Green spoke, as if eager to help her.

"She pulled up the moment I overtook her, sir."

"Very sensible of you," Roger told her drily. He spoke casually so as not to add to her nervousness. "How often have you been here before, Mrs. Margerison?"

The answer came like a reflex action.

"Never. It's the first time."

Roger did not believe that for a moment. When one came to a strange street, one drove slowly, looking about with great care, anxious not to overshoot the house one was looking for. And he had seen the assurance with which she had drawn up; the assurance of familiarity; but he decided this was not the moment to force that issue.

"Why did you come?" he asked next.

"A friend — a friend telephoned and

said he was here, and I so wanted to see him." She had a pleasant speaking voice, and now there was great earnestness in her manner. She even stretched a hand towards him, fragile-looking, beautifully kept.

"Who was the friend?"

"I — I don't know his name, he was a friend of David's."

She had her story off pat; had doubtless had time to think it up when she had been on the run, which meant she had a good, clear mind. Now her soft lips and deep blue eyes seemed to plead with him to believe her. And Green, for some reason, seemed anxious for her; perhaps because she appeared to be so fragile and helpless.

"I see," Roger said. "Sergeant, take Mrs. Margerison to Scotland Yard and have her wait there until I'm back. I'm not charging her yet, if she wants legal advice or a solicitor to be with her next time we talk, that will be in order." He nodded, and half-turned.

"Oh, please!" Angela exclaimed.

Still on the move, he asked: "Please what?"

"Don't make me come to Scotland Yard. I've told you the truth, I swear."

Roger turned round, very slowly, and faced her. He was not only impressively handsome, there was something commanding and yet forbidding in the set of his lips and the hardness in his eyes. The girl-woman's lips quivered and the fear was back in her eyes.

"You are lying," he said icily. "You are quite a bare-faced liar, Mrs. Margerison. I will see you at the Yard."

He turned again, as the girl drew in her breath, almost like a whimper. Venables was in the doorway, head bent to avoid banging it. He looked first over Roger's head to the woman; he had never seen such a beautiful little creature in his life! But quickly his gaze shifted to Roger; and as quickly he dodged to one side to allow the superintendent to pass, then turned to follow him.

As they strode along the passage and into the garden, the girl returned to the car, with Green's hand on the top of her arm, both protectingly and restrainingly. It was almost as if he feared she would pull herself free and make another dash for safety.

But she did not.

Detective Officer Venables watched

West's back and shoulders and the back of his head, noticing the sprinkle of grey in his hair which nevertheless looked flaxen from a distance. He was seeing, as he always did, a dozen things at the same time. He had a remarkable capacity for observation, which came naturally to him, and an almost unbelievably retentive, even photographic mind. These things he knew. What he didn't yet know was how he could best use these qualities in his chosen profession, and so far he hadn't been too impressed by his colleagues. Green, for instance, worked by rule of thumb, missing absolutely nothing and deducing shrewdly from what he saw, but trained mind or not, my God, there was an incredible lot that he didn't see. And most of Venables' seniors, from sergeants through inspectors to superintendents had little time for him. They told him what to do and expected him to do it, and often appeared to take little notice of his extensive and detailed notes; secretly he doubted whether these were read through, and so he grew to doubt whether they were worth making.

At least, no one had told him not to, and so he went on doing them.

He typed his reports, and so was able to keep a carbon copy for himself, for he had discovered even at school that what one knew thoroughly at one period, one could forget, or remember inaccurately, at another. He kept his reports as a detective officer in a loose-leaf folder in his room. Though this one was fairly thin as yet, there were three thick volumes compiled in the three years he had served in the uniformed branch.

When he had realised that he was going to work on an investigation with the renowned "Handsome" West, he had had a fit of the shivers, due entirely to excitement. For West was the man he most admired. In the first place he was perhaps the most successful senior officer at the Yard, and a man whom everybody liked. Well, nearly everybody. He seldom threw his weight about; he sometimes drove his men but never as much as he drove himself. And, his reputation claimed, he treated his men as human beings, not as cyphers.

Venables now knew exactly what that meant, and since West had shown such obviously genuine concern for his cut finger, and since he had taken notice of his observations and not brushed them aside, as Green had, he felt a warm glow whenever he thought of West.

That glow had cooled, for the first time, when he had heard West talk to the woman whom Green had brought back. And it seemed to fade entirely as he saw West's set face, the sternness, even a hint of ruthlessness in his expression. He realised for the first time that West would be a very bad man to cross. And he sensed, without knowing what it was, some extra tension about him now: as if there were other contributing factors to his mood, it wasn't wholly due to the woman.

They reached the back garden, beyond the passage, and West slackened his pace, then suddenly stopped and stared at a spot in the lawn. Venables followed his gaze, and for the first time noticed that some of the turf was slightly raised — as if it had been dug up, and then put down again: there were even marks where some heavy round object had been used to thump the grass down.

And he, Venables, hadn't noticed that before.

3

A HOLE IN THE GROUND

"SEE that?" asked West.
"Yes, sir," said Venables.
"Did you notice it before?"
"No, sir, I'm afraid not."
"What size would you say the patch is?"
Venables gulped, as the other man turned to look at him.
"About six feet by two, sir."
"Coffin-shaped," West remarked.
"Yes, sir."
"Seen any spades on the premises?" asked West.
"Yes, sir — there's a small shed over there." Venables turned and pointed. He was acutely aware of something very sharp about West's manner: he had a sense that he was really seeing the man in action.
"Quicker we dig the better," West said. "Get two spades, will you? Or a fork and a spade."

Venables hurried back to open the door of a wooden shed built against the wall, reached inside to grab a spade hanging upside down from a slanting nail, and then snatched his hand away. *Supposing there were fingerprints on the handle.* He was torn between doing what West had told him, and following his own cautious way. He looked over his shoulder to see West bending down, then squatting on his haunches and looking at the newly-stamped grass. *Supposing any prints on the garden tools were the only ones and so the only clues*, thought Venables. Then he saw West's head jerk upwards. Again, he felt as if he had been caught out looking rather like a fool.

"Hold it!" called West.

"I — er — yes, sir."

"There might be fingerprints," West added.

"That's — that's what suddenly struck me, sir," declared Venables, rejoicing.

"Go and get my box," ordered Roger. "We can make a quick check."

Venables was glowing again, and although he didn't run he went off in a hurry. He disappeared without once looking back. Had he looked back he would have seen that West was smiling, more relaxed than he had been for some time.

In fact, Roger was feeling much more pleased than he could reasonably have hoped. The discovery of Margerison's body had, in itself, been a break: the address had been an even greater one: the behaviour of the girl-wife suggested that she knew more than she had admitted, and before long, she was going to have a very nasty shock indeed. She was going to learn that her husband was dead and might have been murdered.

The human being in Roger responded to this with some disquiet; he had a feeling that the news was going to hit her very hard indeed. But the policeman in him, the detective, could see only the other aspect: that if she came to believe that he had been murdered, then she would want vengeance; and so, she was much more likely to talk. If she kicked her heels at the Yard for an hour or two she would really be in a highly nervous state; and the other news would almost certainly break down her resistance.

It was a cold-blooded way of looking

at the situation: but how else could a policeman look at it?

Venables, for instance.

He liked what he saw of Venables very much indeed. There was something in the young man's appearance which reminded him of one of his two sons: Richard, who was carving out a career in television. It was the dark bushy hair and the clearly defined eyebrows which caused the resemblance, as well as the very quick mind. There were hundreds of good detectives at the Yard, young men especially, but the really outstanding ones were few and far between. It was far too early to say, but Venables certainly had promise: and because of that, Roger had tried him out on the spades. Once he had told the other to go and get them he had squatted down, ostensibly to examine the turf, actually to see what Venables did. He, Roger, had been on the point of calling out to stop him from touching any of the tools, and had felt deep satisfaction when, before the warning had passed his lips, Venables had drawn back as if stung. The way he mumbled: "That's — that's what suddenly struck me, sir," was comical in that it sounded and he looked guilty and apologetic.

It was worth a lot of mistakes to come upon a really top-class detective mind.

Roger's thoughts flashed back to the night of the robbery when he had been called out of bed to go to the docks. There were the high walls, like a prison, the Port of London Authority police on duty, the cobbled roads, the railway lines, the floodlights on the ships being unloaded, the clanking of metal and the hooting of train whistles, the big lorries carrying the huge containers for the liner trains. This shipment of South African gold had been loaded into a lorry, for taking to the Bank of England. Special police, armed guards, every obvious precaution had been taken. What no one had anticipated was that the driver of the lorry was working with the gang of thieves.

He had been David Margerison.

He had given the guard sitting up front with him a doped cigarette: morphine-filled. When the man had lost consciousness he had pulled up at a corner where the rest of his gang had waited. Trusted by the guards at the back, he had called to them through a microphone to say his companion had lost consciousness. They had opened the bulletproof back doors, to investigate: and been overwhelmed by the waiting thieves.

It had been as smooth a coup as any Roger could remember; on a par with the Great Train Robbery, and in some ways carried out more efficiently. Now, he could imagine that the lorry had been brought to this house and unloaded; or more likely, unloaded into smaller vans and brought here in manageable parcels. Gold was one of the heaviest metals to handle.

He had checked every possible angle, would have sworn he had covered everything and everyone; yet he had been careless with Angela Margerison. Oh, he could shift the blame: he could claim, rightly, that he had received the Commander C.I.D.'s approval not to have Angela followed after the first month. But he should not have taken the watch off her. Looking back, he still didn't know why he had. It was one of those inexplicable lapses to which all men are subject, but for it to have happened in this case. . . .

The bullion robbery had coincided with a dearth of news. Headlines ran across every front page, editorials demanded action, the Yard had seldom been under greater pressure. And because he was the Yard's glamour boy and because he was in any case always a target for the Press, he had been featured, first as the man who would track down the perpetrators of a daring robbery, then as the man who had failed. Every week or two a newspaper disinterred the story, creating new sensation upon sensation. One, only a few weeks ago, had asked in its headline:

SHOULD THE YARD'S GLAMOUR BOY RETIRE?

He had never felt less like retiring.

He had never been more conscious of failure, either. After all, if he had had the girl-wife watched she might have led the police to this house while the crooks and the gold had still been here.

He wasn't sure the gold had even *been* here!

Where the devil was Venables with his kit? He felt suddenly chill, shivered, and moved towards the house as Venables appeared, carrying the case which looked so much like a doctor's bag, taking long strides but nevertheless looking over his shoulder at the small window of the inner room.

"Sorry it took so long, sir." With anyone else Roger would have growled: "Why did it?" but he could not, the other's manner was so disarming. "There was a message for you from the Yard. I waited for it over the telephone."

"What message?" asked West.

"Is there any pathologist you would particularly like for the autopsy on the body of David Margerison?"

"Yes," Roger answered. "I would like Dr. Appleby."

Venables gave a broad and happy smile.

"Then that's just right, sir. The message was that it would be Dr. Appleby if you didn't call back within half an hour."

Roger grunted.

He took the case, put it on top of a metal coal bunker, and opened it, taking out a bottle of grey dusting powder — old-fashioned Fuller's Earth — and a pair of paint brushes, both camel hair. He dusted the handle of the fork and spade, and handed one brush to Venables, who drew it gently over the shiny part of the handle, he ran the brush over the shaft, just as carefully.

Roger did the same to the spade, with the same care.

By the time he was half through he felt sure of the final result, but he finished before he spoke.

"Nothing here."

"Nor here, sir."

"Wiped clean," remarked Roger. "Your professional job again."

"Couldn't have been much more thorough, sir, could it? But — " Venables broke off, as Roger picked up the spade and moved towards the grass.

"But what?" asked Roger.

"Er — doesn't matter, sir."

"I'd still like to hear."

"I was thinking of Gross, sir. And Glaister."

"Ah," said Roger. "The authorities."

"They *are* pretty good, sir, aren't they?"

"First-class."

"And they both say virtually the same thing, that the criminal always leaves *some* clue behind. I know it sounds sententious, but they do, sir."

"Like all clichés, it's based on truth," Roger remarked.

"Absolutely, sir!" Venables gave his most expansive grin yet, and dug the fork into the ground. Roger made a line with the spade, around the coffin-sized piece of grass, and then began to dig. He rather enjoyed it. The earth was soft, and the spade went in fairly easily. He took off half a dozen sods, and then paused.

"Notice that?" he asked.

"They've been cut and put down recently, sir."

"Yes. Our man's mistake, perhaps." Roger now began to dig deeper, acutely aware of the speed with which Venables dug, lifting turf after turf. Then suddenly a man came hurrying.

"Here, sir! Let me do that!" It was Green, who seemed outraged that Roger should be digging. He almost pushed Roger aside in his eagerness to take the spade. He looked excited, too, and he turned to Roger, one foot on the shoulder of the spade itself. "I've had the same story from three neighbours, sir."

"Can you whistle and ride?" asked Roger.

"Eh? Oh — dig and talk at the same time!" Green gave a guffaw and dug deep. "Yes, sir — haven't heard that phrase for a long time! These people who lived here were thought by the neighbours to be night-workers. Two of them drove lorries which were sometimes parked outside. Kept themselves very much to themselves, sir, the neighbours saw very little of them."

"That figures," Roger said.

"Undercover work, sir!"

"Who did the gardening?" Roger asked.

Without a moment's hesitation, almost as if he gave it no thought at all, Green answered: "The women, sir, two of them. No one ever saw the men in the garden except for a few minutes at a time."

All the while, Green dug; and he might have been a trained gardener, even a grave digger, for he drove the spade in with smooth precision, his movements neat and powerful. The soil was nearly black. At the other end of the patch,

Venables was now doing little more than scratch the surface. Neither the rhythm of Green's digging nor the rhythm of his reporting was disturbed.

"You say three neighbours all said the same thing?"

"Pretty well, sir. I've got the answers down, verbatim." For the first time Green paused, to wipe his forehead with his sleeve. "Any idea what we're digging for?"

"Anything from gold bullion to a body, I should think."

Green said, wiping his forehead with the same sleeve and speaking with exactly the same almost casual deliberation as he had before: "A body is more likely, I'd say."

Roger went tense.

"What makes you think so?"

"Not often my nose deceives me," said Green. "Don't you notice the stench?"

Roger looked down at the hole the other man had dug, saw nothing but the dark earth, but fancied that there was a faint odour of decay. Green bent down to sniff, distended his nostrils with the delicacy of a rabbit. Then he drew back.

"It's decaying flesh all right," he declared. "We ought to dig very carefully now."

"Yes," Roger said. "We'd better have more tools and more men. Better have the photographer here, too, quickly. Go and fix it, will you?" Green slammed the spade into the side of a flower bed, and went off with a "Right, sir!" flung over his shoulder. He did not appear to glance at Venables but that might have been quite deliberate.

For Venables was leaning heavily on the handle of his fork. His face was a greenish-grey; he looked as if he would faint at any moment. He did not glance up as Roger called his name, then sprang forward to save him from falling.

4
WEAKNESS

VENABLES appeared to have fainted. His body was heavy against Roger, his arms drooped, his knees were bent. Roger eased him away from the fork on which he was leaning, and half-dragged, half-carried him towards the house. By the shed was a wooden bench, and Roger sat the man on it. He was coming round, and his eyes were flickering but his colour was still very bad. He muttered something which sounded like "Sorry". Roger didn't respond. Already his relationship with this man was more like father-to-son than senior police officer to rookie.

Venables sat more upright.

"I'm — I'm terribly sorry, sir."

"Does this kind of thing always affect you this way?"

"The — the stench does, yes, sir. The sight of blood doesn't worry me, it — it's just the stench." He looked at Roger with piteous gaze. "It — it needn't ruin my career, need it?"

Roger answered: "It could, Venables." He hated saying that but there was no point in lying. "Unless you can control it."

"I — I try to, sir. Desperately."

"I'm sure you do. One of the best detectives I've ever known, an American from Chicago, couldn't stand the sight of blood when he first signed on with the police. He's a senior police officer now."

Venables gave a ghastly smile.

"Then — there — there's some hope, sir!"

"Yes. Who knows about this problem?"

"Not — not many people, sir."

"Anyone on the Force?"

"No," Venables answered. "My — my mother and my brother, they know. My mother tried to keep me out of the police because of it, she said that it would prove to be my Achilles heel."

"She might not have wanted you to join the police," Roger remarked drily.

"Oh, it wasn't that, sir. I — oh, hell! What's the use of talking? I'm sure to come across this kind of thing from time to time, aren't I?"

"Yes," Roger answered. "And if you

want to stay in the C.I.D., you're going to have to overcome it at least as far as showing it is concerned. How are you now?"

"Better, sir, much better." Then belatedly: "Thank you."

"Then I want you to take the splinter of glass you cut yourself on, back to the Yard," Roger said. "Take it direct to the laboratory to see if they can identify the glass in any way — what utensil it was before it was broken, for instance. And when you're through with the glass, make out a report on what you've done and seen today, in as much detail as you can. Can you type?"

"Oh, yes, sir!"

"Then type it," Roger ordered. He took the small plastic envelope which contained the splinter of glass from his pocket and handed it to Venables, who placed it with great care into his breast pocket. Then he stood up. His colour was almost normal and his eyes were bright again: eager.

"Thank you *very* much, sir. I'll — I'll fight this weakness if I possibly can, sir. Being in the C.I.D. is a tremendous thing to me. I've always been crazy about detection. I read all the thrillers I can lay my hands on, especially the puzzle kind, and I don't think I've missed a police officer's biography or autobiography, sir, ever. And I know all the authorities, like Gross and Glaister and Svensen and — " He broke off, very abruptly, and straightened up to his full height. "Goodness knows what's got into me, I can't stop talking. I'm *very* sorry."

Roger knew exactly what had got into him: a kind of shock and emotional upset. He had shown himself in his greatest weakness to a man whom he probably regarded as an idol. And to cover an excess of nervousness, he talked on and on. Now, however, he turned and strode off, those big feet planting themselves down with such softness, his hands almost rigid at his sides. He disappeared, with a glance through the window of the small room.

Roger did not follow; if there had been any great discovery he would have been told. He moved back to the place where the digging had started. There was a faint odour of decay but it certainly wasn't overpowering. It would be a pity if Venables was really over-sensitive to it.

Then, Green arrived, with two more men and two more spades. They began to dig, with speed but also with great care. Before long they uncovered some brown canvas which was already rotting; and when they unrolled this they discovered, inside it, the body of a man.

What followed wasn't one of the pleasant jobs, but it had to be done. By now a full murder investigation team was on the spot from the West London Division. Roger knew Carr, the man in charge of the team, a Chief Inspector who would do everything which had to be done with speed and efficiency.

"If necessary, take the body out through the next door garden," Roger said. "The less we trample that house the better."

"I'll fix something," Carr promised. "What's it about, sir?"

"Bullion," answered Roger simply.

"Still on that one, are you, sir?" Carr was a man in his middle-forties, with short black hair, a dark jowl, and fierce-looking, amber-coloured eyes. "What happens if the Press turns up?"

"Refer them to me."

"Right." Carr spoke as if that would be a pleasure.

He went on to superintend the digging, and to search the garden, while Roger moved inside. Four men, a crowd in that small room, had levered up a dozen or so tiles of the floor where the so far unidentified machine had stood, finding a solid concrete bed underneath. This had obviously been here for some time, and once several pieces of heavy kitchen equipment had been here; labels on the walls showed: Deep Freeze — Refrigerator — Dishwasher — Stove.

"Not many of these old houses are fitted with a 30 amp current to feed a single phase motor so that you could drive a lathe," one of the detectives remarked.

"Sure there was a lathe?" asked Roger.

"Something of that kind was stuck down, sir. None of the kitchen stuff was, though, but you can see marks where it stood. The lathe was a later date — you can see where it was stuck over the places where the other stuff had been."

Roger bent down and studied the marks, little more than shadows, which only a remarkably thorough man would have noticed.

"Nice work," he said warmly.

"Thank you, sir."

"Have we anything else?" asked Roger.

One man was sieving the small pieces and the dust which had gone through the first mesh. It might be an hour, even two or three, before they had the rest of the tiles up.

On a trestle table in the big room which had been empty when he had first seen Venables, were a dozen little plastic bags. Most contained dust. Others contained pins, pieces of broken nails and tacks, the metal tip of a bootlace. Each envelope was marked: front room, kitchen, middle room, downstairs cloakroom, bedroom 1, bedroom 2, and so on. On that table, in envelopes little larger than those used in ordinary correspondence, were all the oddments found after a thorough search of 17, Lyon Avenue.

"A professional job," Venables had said.

It was the most thorough job of cleaning Roger had ever come across, and he had no doubt at all that it had been done to remove all the clues which might have been left behind.

The time had come to talk to Angela Margerison.

The car in which he had been brought here, with Green, was now parked a little farther up the road. A few people stood about in idle curiosity but no one had yet arrived from the newspapers. The constable on duty sprang to attention as Roger appeared.

"Do you know Sergeant Green?" Roger asked.

"Yes, sir — by sight, that is."

"Tell him I've taken the car, he'll need to get a lift back to the Yard," Roger said.

"I'll see to it, sir." The policeman opened the door of the driving seat side, and Roger drove off almost at once; even a delay of a few seconds might have him caught by newspapermen and he did not want to answer questions.

It was half past one. Time hadn't gone so quickly as it might with so much happening. He felt peckish, but food could wait: in fact he was more thirsty than hungry. Early afternoon traffic was quite heavy, and he found little inclination for coping with the heavy trucks and the impatient drivers. Why was it that the smaller the car the more its driver seemed to demand of it? A scarlet Mini passed within inches of his nearside wing, a tow-headed youth at the wheel. A girl on the pavement darted back to safety; she reminded Roger of Angela Margerison. A policeman on the far side of the road stared after the scarlet Mini, presumably memorising the number, for that really had been a case of dangerous driving. Roger thought censoriously that it was a miracle that there weren't far more road casualties.

He cut through the back streets behind Harrods until he reached the one-way system of roads about Victoria, which, having spent his childhood in this area, always confused him a little. When he reached Broadway, just off Victoria Street, and saw the tall modern building of glass and concrete, the same impression of strangeness remained. The difference between this and the "old" New Scotland Yard was so great that at times he resented it, despite the greater light and the square spaciousness of the rooms and the aids to efficiency. The Information Room and the new Records Department really *were* something!

A detective sergeant of the Criminal Investigation Department was just coming out of the Victoria Street entrance as Roger drew up.

"On an urgent job?" asked Roger.

"Not desperately, sir." The freckled face had a pleasant expression.

"Then put this car away for me, will you?" Roger got out and before the car had moved from the kerb was inside the wide passage. There was no one at all in sight. He went up alone in a large, self-operated lift to the fourth floor, and along to his own office, which overlooked Victoria Street rooftops and, in the distance, the dome of the Tate Gallery.

There were two messages on his desk.

Coppell, the Commander C.I.D., wanted to see him as soon as he got in. And Dr. Appleby, the pathologist, had telephoned. Appleby couldn't have finished the autopsy yet; there was hardly time for him to have started. There was a telephone number: not Appleby's home or office. He pulled one of three telephones on his desk closer and dialled the number. It rang for a long time, and Roger was about to replace the receiver when the ringing sound broke. A man with a rather light, questioning voice answered.

"Who is that?"

It was Appleby himself, one of the youngest and perhaps the ablest of the Home Office team of pathologists. The years had made him and Roger good friends; had they been able to see more of each other they would have been much closer.

"Roger West," Roger answered.

"Oh. H-H-Handsome. Glad you c-caught me, I was on my w-w-way out. H-had a bit of d-d-domestic trouble, had to leave the cadaver on the b-b-bench. It will be three or four hours before I c-c-can g-g-get back to the job. S-s-sorry."

"Well, it can't be helped," Roger said, trying not to sound as disappointed as he felt.

"W-won't be a m-m-minute longer than I m-m-must," promised Appleby, and then added with a kind of sting in the tail characteristic of him: "Chap didn't die by drowning, that's a fact."

Roger's heart leapt.

"Can I take that as positive?"

"Ab-ab-absolutely," Appleby assured him. " 'Bye."

The telephone at the other end went dead. Roger replaced his more slowly. If Margerison hadn't died by drowning then the possibility of suicide became even more remote; how like Appleby to get the essentials first. Roger made a note on a sheet of paper on which he had already jotted down the time of the call from Thames Division, the finding of the body and who he had sent to the house in Lyon Avenue, then picked up the middle of the three telephones. It was white, and used for internal use. The one on which he had called Appleby was black; the third, connected to the Yard's switchboard, was grey. He dialled the Commander's number, and immediately a woman's voice, rich and plummy, answered.

"Mr. Coppell's office."

"This is West," Roger said. This particular woman nearly always managed to irritate him, for she guarded her boss too well and threw her own weight about too much. But this morning she was prompt and pleasant.

"Oh, yes, Mr. West, one moment please." The moment grew into several but then Coppell with his deep, gruff voice came on. Coppell had been thrust into the job of Assistant Commissioner several years ago, and no one had expected him to keep the job for long. A mixture of circumstances and his own dogged courage had combined to keep him in it; he was far from being a good A.C. but now the Yard was used to him.

"How did you get on at Chiswick?" Coppell demanded without preamble.

"Another body," Roger answered mildly.

"My God!" Coppell choked, and then he added sharply: "Any gold?"

"Hardly a speck of dust," Roger answered. "I've never seen a place cleaned up so well — it even had a wax polish. Whoever was there meant to be as sure as possible that we couldn't find a clue."

"Did you?" Coppell almost barked.

"The only one I'm sure about is a splinter of glass," Roger replied, and then drew a deep breath. Coppell was breathing heavily into the telephone, but momentarily silent. He was extremely sensitive about the bullion robbery and the complete getaway, and he would react badly to news of a mistake. "One other thing is both good and bad," he went on.

"Oh. What?"

"We caught Margerison's wife — she was obviously coming to the house."

There was a long pause, and the heavy breathing stopped, as if Coppell was holding his breath. Then:

"So if we'd kept her under surveillance she might have led us there while the place was still occupied."

"Yes," Roger agreed, and drew in a deep breath. "I couldn't have made a bigger mistake."

"Too bloody right you couldn't." Coppell growled. He was silent again, and then went on: "This will have to go in my weekly Bullion case report to the Commissioner. You know that, don't you?"

"Of course."

"They'll want my neck as well as yours," Coppell complained, and then added with a snort of sound: "So you've two necks to save, Handsome. Where's this woman — Angela Margerison, isn't she?"

"That's right. She's being held in the waiting room. I'm going down to see her now."

"Before you let her go, consult me, won't you?" said Coppell with heavy sarcasm. He rang off, saving Roger from the need to reply, and for the second time Roger put his receiver down slowly and deliberately. Coppell's reaction could have been a lot worse, but it was bad enough; and it was news to Roger that he still had to put in a weekly report on the Bullion Case. He got up, frowning, and was at the door when a telephone bell rang — the shrill one from the internal telephone which could be connected to police cars through *Information*. He strode back and picked it up.

"West."

"It's Detective Sergeant Green here, sir," Green said, with excitement tautening his voice. "We've got the body up, sir. Haven't identified it yet. Naked, with one or two superficial wounds. Mr. Carr would like to know, do you want it sent to Dr. Appleby?"

"Yes," Roger answered, sure that this wasn't what affected the usually stolid sergeant's voice. "Anything else, Green?"

"Yes, sir," Green declared. "We've found *two* gold shavings behind the skirting of the wall where that machine used to stand. Absolutely no doubt about it, they're gold, could easily have been off a gold bar, sir. Shall I bring them right over?"

"Yes. Don't lose a minute," Roger urged with tremendous relief. "Take them to the laboratory, and wait until I come, will you?" He rang off on Green's cheerful "Yes, sir!" and moved slowly towards the door. The deep satisfaction at the discovery of the gold was offset by the fact that only a week ago, a police raid might have caught all of the gang who lived there — and the gold as well.

And all because he had allowed himself to be fooled by the girl-wife — now a girl-widow — whom he was going to see.

Well, she wouldn't fool him again.

5

ANGELA MARGERISON

THE waiting or interview room where Angela Margerison sat was one of several equipped with one-way win-windows. Anyone inside could be seen from outside, but they couldn't see out, had no idea they were being observed. Angela was in an upright armchair, not too comfortable, and a policewoman sat in a similar armchair, leafing through a copy of the *Police Gazette*. Roger pressed a button, to announce his arrival, and the policewoman rose at once. Angela seemed to stiffen as she turned her head towards the door.

Roger went in.

"Good-afternoon, sir," the policewoman said.

"Good-afternoon. Do you take shorthand, officer?"

"Yes, sir."

"I'd like a verbatim report of this interview, please." Roger spoke stiffly, all the time looking at Angela Margerison, who seemed now to be nothing but eyes. Another chair was at hand but he preferred to stand. "We have the formal details of Mrs. Margerison's full name, address and status, haven't we?"

The policewoman tapped her notebook. "Yes, sir."

"Has Mrs. Margerison been given any information?"

"None, sir. She was escorted here by Detective Sergeant Green and I have been with her since her arrival. No information has been passed on to her."

Roger nodded, still looking at the tiny woman who shrank back in her chair. There was something about her which was exceptionally appealing, and he had an unpleasant certainty that he was going to hurt her very much indeed with the news of her husband's death. His intention, on his way down, had been to tell her bluntly, even brutally, so as to weaken her resistance and persuade her to talk. But there was something so fragile about her; and a kind of innocence too. It was easy to warn himself that she had taken him in before; as useless to try to forget that she was a woman about to be given a heavy blow: a cruel enough hurt in itself.

So, he drew up a chair and sat down.

"Mrs. Margerison," he said. "You went to the house in Lyon Avenue hoping to see your husband, didn't you?"

She gave no answer.

"Had you been there before?" he asked, and when she didn't reply he went on: "The neighbours there are extremely observant and were very curious about the new people at Number 17. There is no doubt at all that if they were here with us they would recognise you as a frequent caller." There *was* doubt, but it was a fair enough assumption. He gave her long enough to understand what he had said, and then asked again: "*Had* you been there before?"

"Yes," she managed to say in a voice it was difficult to hear.

"To see your husband?"

"Yes." Her voice was still muted, and her eyes seemed to burn.

"How often did you go there?"

"Once — once a week."

"When did you start these visits?"

"As — as soon as it was certain you weren't having me watched," she answered simply, and she could not know how barbed that answer was for Roger.

"Are you used to being followed by the police?" he asked wryly.

Her eyes suddenly burst into flame; life seemed to pour back into her, and her voice was clear and positive as she replied. "Oh, *no*!"

"Then how did you know when we stopped watching?"

She didn't answer at first.

There had been so many pauses in this dialogue that the policewoman could have had no difficulty in keeping up with her notes, and she sat very still in the corner. Roger had forgotten her until this moment, when he glanced across and asked:

"Will you have some coffee sent in, please?"

"Yes, sir." The woman picked up a telephone, and Roger turned back to Angela. That "Oh, *no*!" seemed to hover still about her head. He waited long enough for the coffee to be ordered before asking:

"Then how did you know you had been followed and then the men had been withdrawn?"

"I — I telephoned David."

"Where?"

"At — at that house in Lyon Avenue. But I only had the number at first, I didn't know where it was. And — and I didn't know anything when you were questioning me, I promise I didn't lie to you. It wasn't for over a month that I had a telephone call from David. *He* told me the address: *and* he told me I could go and see him every week. He — he usually telephoned me the day before. He missed this week, I had to come and find out why." Now she was beginning to talk not only freely but fast, and Roger made no attempt to slow her down. "Sometimes I had lunch and spent the afternoon and the evening there, it — it was wonderful!" She threw that out almost in defiance, and as if she expected to be rebuked for taking pleasure in these visits to her husband. Suddenly, she sprang to her feet and began to walk about the room. "It *was* wonderful! It's always wonderful with David, those awful weeks when I couldn't see him were terrible, the worst time I've ever had in my life. And he didn't tell me anything about what he'd done. He — he just made me feel as if I were the only person in the world who mattered to him! He *did*!" She stopped just in front of Roger, glaring wild defiance. "I don't care what he's done, I don't care what you think he is, he's the most wonderful man who ever lived!"

And her tone, her manner, her poise all seemed to cry: "And don't you dare say that he isn't!"

And the "most wonderful man who ever lived" was dead.

Roger felt a heavy weight of depression, a touch of nausea. Her reaction to hearing the brutal truth was going to be very bad indeed. The recollection that he had come here intending to use the husband's death to make her talk turned sour on him, he wished he were anywhere but here, wished anyone but he had this job to do. For he believed all she had said: despite his sense of having been fooled before, he believed her now. It wasn't her fault that he had withdrawn the watch, and no amount of wishing he hadn't would help.

But she had told him one thing, perhaps without realising it: someone else had been watching her — someone who had realised how closely she had been kept under surveillance for a while, and when the police had withdrawn. Well, he needed no telling that the bullion robbers were very shrewd and efficient, they were probably very experienced in police-watching, too.

There was a tap at the door, and a woman in a blue smock brought in a laden tray: coffee, milk, biscuits. She did not look at Angela but only at West, put the tray down, said: "There you are, sir," and went out on his: "Thanks." That was mechanical, he was thinking only of Angela and the news he had to break, and whether he should ask more questions now or tell her about her husband and then put the questions to which he must have the answers.

It was a heartbreaking decision to have to make.

The obvious thing was to ask now, but if he did that, the shock effect of the news might be greater; and once she had recovered a little she would understand that he must have been killed by his accomplices: that her revenge could only come by telling everything she knew of them.

Slowly, he became aware of a change in her expression and in her manner. She stared at him intently and with a dawning horror. He was puzzled; and suddenly wondered if this were some trick — whether he had been fooled yet again by her look of innocence.

"What is it?" she asked tensely.

"What is what?"

"What made you look like that?"

He didn't answer, but he understood what had prompted the question. His expression had been too easy to read, the compassion he felt showing clearly. She was ultra-sensitive about her husband, and the way she had talked *had* filled him with dread at the thought of telling her.

"What is it?" she cried again. "What's the matter?"

This was the moment when he had to tell her; there was no choice at all.

He put his hands out towards her. Out of the corner of his eye he saw the police officer stand up; he could not see her expression clearly but had a sense that she was aware of the coming crisis.

Angela did not take his hands, but backed a pace and almost screamed: *"What is the matter?"*

"Mrs. Margerison," Roger said, huskily, "I am very, very sorry."

"Sorry!" she echoed wildly. "What do you mean, *sorry*? What's happened?"

He said: "Your husband is dead. We learned that this morning. I am — dreadfully sorry."

Now her expression changed. Her eyes narrowed. Her lips closed and went into a a thin line; the little face became not pretty but spiteful — not young but old.

"You're lying!" she spat.

"I wish I was."

"You're lying! You're trying to make me talk, and I won't. I won't, I *won't*! You're lying to me!"

"He's dead," Roger insisted. "You must believe that."

"It's a wicked lie!"

"His body was found in the Thames this morning."

"No!" she gasped, and now the colour drained from her cheeks. "No, I don't believe you. It's not true!"

"We think he was murdered," Roger stated, as flatly as he could.

"*You're lying to me!*" she screamed again — and then without the slightest warning she flung herself at him and before he had a chance to defend himself, she had struck him across the face, scratching his cheek; she kept beating at him as he put out an arm to restrain her. She was gasping and screaming on a suffocating note, but as the policewoman jumped up the outburst began to ebb. The policewoman reached her and put an arm round her shoulders. Angela Margerison buried her face in her hands.

Words came, almost unintelligible: "He's not dead. Tell me he's not."

Roger said heavily: "I'm sorry, truly sorry."

"Oh, no," she gasped. "Not David." Then her voice rose again: "He can't be dead."

For one moment she drew her hands from her face, to look at Roger as if searching for the truth. And what she read made her bury her face in her hands again, and begin to sob. At first, only her shoulders moved, but slowly the crying racked her whole body. The policewoman shifted her stance, cradling and supporting her, then spoke in a low-pitched voice.

"I don't think she'll be able to talk for a while, sir."

"No," Roger agreed. "No. Do you need a doctor?"

"It might be wise, sir, but I'd rather stay here with her for a few minutes, if that's all right with you."

"Yes," Roger said, and after a pause, went on: "What is your name?"

"Nicholson, sir. Rose Nicholson."

"Do what you think best," Roger said, and went on with more effort than he had dreamt would be needed: "You know that we may have to hold her, don't you?"

"Yes."

"I'll be in my office," Roger said. "Let me know when she's better and if we need a doctor."

"Very good, sir."

"We certainly need to know everything she can tell us about the house where she saw her husband," Roger said. "We now know that two people who were at the house are dead. It is getting very ugly. We need to know how many she saw, we want descriptions, names, absolutely everything she can tell us, and every minute's delay might be serious."

The policewoman said, pleadingly: "I *do* understand, sir."

Roger nodded and went out.

He was back in his office before he

realised that he'd had no coffee or biscuits, and his headache and nausea might be due simply to the fact that he had eaten nothing since an early breakfast, consisting only of toast and marmalade, with strong coffee. He went along the passage and up to the big canteen on the fifth floor. Only one section and one cafeteria here was open. At a table near the windows of the long room was Coppell and another chief superintendent; senior officers often ate here instead of in their special dining-room on the floor above. Coppell saw him but didn't beckon, so he was concentrating on another case. Roger took some soup, and some sausages and mashed potatoes standing on a hotplate. He put a roll and some butter on his tray, added coffee, and went to a seat at the far end of the room.

At first, he felt almost too queasy to eat, but once he started he felt better. What was the matter with him? First Venables, then the uniformed man in Lyon Avenue, then Angela Margerison: was he reacting far too emotionally to people? He ate and pondered and asked himself what else he could have done: and he didn't see any other course. That made him feel better. He heard a heavy tread behind him and looked round, expecting to see Coppell. Instead, it was a man of Coppell's build but very different in appearance: sandy-haired, fresh-complexioned, the kind of man and face which would be good in television advertisements for fresh farm produce.

It was Chief Inspector Jacob Smythe, from the laboratory. In civil life he would be Professor Smythe.

"Hallo, Handsome. Feeling solitary?" Smythe had a tray in his hand, too.

"Yes. Sit down, Jake."

He shifted some things from the other side of the table, making room for Smythe to put his tray down: it was heavily laden with steak, eggs, chips and a big slice of suet pudding topped with treacle.

"Peckish?" asked Roger.

"Starving. You don't think I eat like this every day, do you? I will say they've got a couple of good cooks here at the moment. Ever reflect that cops used to go to the cooks of big houses to get a square meal? Ah, me, how things change." He speared half a dozen chips. "Ah! Not re-fried, thank God." He cut a piece of tender-looking steak, and his expression was positively beatific. "What a lucky man you are," he went on.

Roger, watching Smythe eating, hardly took in the significance of the last remark, then suddenly realised what the other had said.

"If I'm lucky, I'd like to meet an unlucky man," he said.

"Still got your head bloodied from bullion?" asked Smythe, knowingly. "Well, you're still lucky, Handsome. You could have brought me a sliver of glass from a hundred sources which I couldn't identify, but that long streak Venables brought me a piece I *can* help to identify. How about that?" he demanded, and placed another juicy piece of steak into his mouth.

6

CLUE?

ROGER'S heart leapt as it hadn't for a long time, but he concealed his excitement, sipped coffee which was now only lukewarm, and then remarked:

"So you're earning your keep."

"Now we'll see if you can earn yours," retorted Smythe.

"What do I have to do?"

"This is a particular type of glass — I will spare you the technicalities," Smythe told him. "It's sufficient to say that it can stand extraordinarily high temperatures without any danger of cracking. For the most part it is used industrially, particularly in experimental laboratories, and it has a singular toughness. The actual glass is mainly made by one firm, near Sheffield, this piece came from a certain kind of container or test tube or flask made by one of several firms in the country which used the product. See," he almost jeered, "I'm already doing half your job for you."

"Are you really sure — we can easily find out who made the thing the splinter came from?"

"Yes. And the manufacturers sell mostly to the trade, and will know who bought this particular article. The number of places where this glass is likely to be used is very restricted — it's expensive and in an experimental stage. Presumably you need to know where this one came from or you wouldn't have sent Venables over with a tale of such urgency."

So Venables had put on all the pressure he possibly could.

"Oh, we certainly need it," Roger affirmed.

"What's the case?" enquired Smythe, revealing that he had been fighting back his curiosity. Before Roger could answer, he added jestingly: "Couldn't be the Bullion Boys, could it?"

Very slowly, Roger nodded; and as he nodded Smythe's grin faded and he took on a wholly serious, almost a sombre expression. He thrust his underlip forward in a Churchillian manner, and for the first time seemed oblivious to the food in front of him.

At last, he announced: "Well, I will say you don't give up."

"It won't give me up," Roger retorted, and told Smythe enough to put him in the picture. Then he got up with a "Many thanks, Jake. You'll let Venables have the names of the manufacturers and users of that particular glass, won't you?" and went off.

Coppell was still at the table with the same officer, and this time he looked up and beckoned. Roger went over, momentarily afraid that Coppell might make some remark which would go round the Yard as if on wheels: Coppell could be very cutting. He looked older, Roger noticed; the Commander C.I.D.'s job took a lot out of a man and Coppell often made heavy weather of his responsibilities.

"How'd you get on with Margerison's wife?" he asked.

"She gave some information before I told her about her husband," Roger answered. "Then she collapsed."

Coppell chewed his underlip before asking aggressively: "Did you have to tell her?"

"Sooner or later."

"Was that the right time?" Coppell demanded.

Roger said: "It seemed to me the right time."

Their voices were so low that no one but the man with Coppell, Detective Superintendent Wall, could possibly hear, but most of the men and the two or three women in the canteen were watching, either covertly or openly. There was something in Coppell's make-up which caused resentment in a lot of men, especially senior officers. He and Roger had been in conflict several times, at least twice when an open clash would have forced Roger's resignation, but each time Coppell had shown the better side of his nature. But that never seemed to last for long. There was something in Roger which easily riled him.

"Where is she now?" Coppell asked.

"With Police Officer Nicholson — Rose Nicholson. She's in a pretty bad way."

"Well, don't let her do away with herself," Coppell said roughly. "We need her for questioning." He nodded dismissal. Roger, already taut with resentment, turned away. Then, in a low pitched voice, Coppell went on: "Soft in the heart, soft in the head, that's the trouble."

Roger stopped in his tracks.

There was Jake Smythe, watching; and three or four chief inspectors and several detective sergeants as well as a dozen men from the civil branch. A waitress dropped a piece of cutlery; it sounded like a car crash, the silence in the canteen was so intense. Everyone was staring at Roger, Coppell perhaps more intently than anyone else. Wall, out of Coppell's line of vision, shook his head slightly and looked very concerned; obviously he was desperately anxious that Roger should not show his resentment.

Roger, said, in a clear, carrying voice: "What I would like, sir, is to see that Mrs. Margerison gets the utmost help and attention, preferably in a nursing home overnight. I don't think it will help if I push her too hard now. Anything she says could be considered under duress, and if we ever get to court with this case, defence counsel will make good use of that."

Coppell was so surprised that he jerked right back in his chair.

"Oh," he said. "That's what you think, is it?"

"Yes," Roger said. "From what I've seen of the girl, she could easily be tipped over into hysteria. She's been living on her nerves for a long time and if we're going to get any help from her we'll have to see her through this bad patch." He drew a deep breath. "May I send her to Dr. Fitzpatrick if it seems necessary?"

Fitzpatrick was a Yard consultant on psychiatry.

Coppell was beginning to glare, obviously realising that Roger had swung over to attack in front of an audience who might well carry the story around.

Then, suddenly, the Commander gave a ferocious grin, and boomed: "Right. Get Fitzpatrick, get whoever you like, but keep her for the witness box — keep her out of Appleby's department."

Roger was already smiling. Wall was also smiling and relaxed, everyone seemed free from tension, as if none had ever existed. Roger brought himself up to attention.

"Thank you, sir," he said, and turned and walked out.

"Mr. West," a woman said on the internal telephone as soon as Roger reached his office. It was twenty minutes since he had left Coppell, everyone who could stop him to ask questions did so. Rumour that he was at last on the track of the bullion robbers was spreading, and creating a rare sense of excitement at the Yard.

"Speaking," Roger said into the telephone.

"It's Police Officer Nicholson here, sir."

"How is Mrs. Margerison?"

"I'm not at all happy about her, sir. She's gone absolutely quiet. She doesn't seem to see or hear anything. You did say get her to a nursing home, didn't you?"

"Yes. Has Sister seen her?"

"She's with her now."

"Send her to Dr. Fitzpatrick's place and ask him to see her as soon as he can," ordered Roger. "If Sister needs an authority, I'll sign it. The Commander would, if necessary. And Nicholson — "

"Yes, sir?"

"When are you due off duty?"

"Eight o'clock, sir, but I can stay on if necessary."

"Stay in Mrs. Margerison's room and fix a relief when you go off duty," Roger ordered. "You know what we need to learn from her. But be guided by Dr. Fitzpatrick." He rang off on Rose Nicholson's "Very good, sir," and then sat back and tried to relax.

He felt as if he had been running since he had come to the Yard this morning, and in a way he had. He needed not so much rest as time to collect his thoughts, to dwell on all that had happened and to get everything in its right perspective. Sitting here, that would probably be impossible; and as if to prove it, the direct line telephone bell rang. So someone who knew about that number was calling from outside the Yard, and few calls except emergencies came on the line.

He did not want to cope with another emergency at the moment.

He picked up the receiver, and barked: "West."

"M-m-my," said Appleby. "You are in a tiz."

"Never mind my tiz," Roger said gruffly. "What have you got for me?"

"In-in-invitation to d-d-dinner," said Appleby, unexpectedly. "If you can b-b-bear to discuss grisly details over the soup."

"I think I can cope," Roger said quite lightly. And more seriously: "I'd like that very much. If it's not a nuisance for Dot."

"Er — D-D-Dot won't be here," Appleby said. "Seven o'clock, just you and me, same place. 'Bye." Before Roger could say another word the line went dead, and Roger, feeling much more himself, was glad that he hadn't gone somewhere else to ponder. He drew a jotting pad to him and began to make notes, soon becoming absorbed in what he was doing. No one came in, the telephone didn't ring for over half an hour, and when it did was only a social call: would he and Janet be going to the Chelsea Divisional Dinner Dance? If so, would they join the caller and his wife?

"Glad to," Roger said. "And how about having Dan Appleby and his wife?"

"Done," said the other man, and rang off.

Roger made a note in his diary, and then returned to the Bullion Case. He needed to know how many people had been at the house: so far he knew of the man who appeared occasionally in the garden, Margerison, and the two women. He needed Green's report on the statements made by the neighbours at Lyon Avenue. He needed to know how long Margerison had been dead; he needed to know the identity of the other dead man and the approximate time of his death, too. Now he began to ask himself other questions: *why* had the men been killed? If Margerison's body hadn't been found with that address in the pocket, the police wouldn't have had a clue about the house in Lyon Avenue.

His exchange telephone rang suddenly, startling him. He snatched the receiver up.

"West."

"This is Charley Baker of South West," said a voice with a faint North Country accent. "There's been an attack on a police car in Marley Street, just outside the Marley Nursing Home. Two women in in the car are injured, one of them — Police Officer Nicholson — badly."

Rose Nicholson had joined the Metropolitan Police Force out of a sense of mission, rather than because she was particularly enthusiastic about the police. For several years she had been a probation officer in the East End of London and she had come to the conclusion that as a policewoman, she could do more good. And in many ways, she had proved that she could.

The case of Angela Margerison differed from most, in which girls from bad homes or with no homes at all were in desperate need of help, advice and above all, understanding and friendship. This doll-like but very lovely woman was obviously well endowed with this world's goods, and she was suffering from the strain of several months of anxiety and now, severe shock. She, Rose, was grateful to West for the chance he had given her, and as soon as she heard what could be done she had arranged for a patrol car to take her and the stricken woman to the Marley Nursing Home, only a mile from New Scotland Yard.

She knew the driver, a man from the South Western Division.

Angela's body sagged heavily against her. The girl seemed to be in a coma rather than suffering from shock. Traffic was heavy and the journey slow, but that did not worry Rose unduly; once they were at the nursing home there would be a doctor, nurses, sedation — anything she needed.

A small green car cut across the front of a taxi, making it brake sharply; she could hear the taxi driver's voice as he yelled abuse.

The errant car then turned the corner into Marley Street, where there was little traffic. The police car, behind it, pulled into the kerb, very gently. At the same moment the small car swung round in a wide circle, and Rose Nicholson saw a man next to the driver.

He had a cap, pulled low over his eyes.

He had a pistol in his hand.

He was only a few yards away when he fired into the car. The windows splintered and glass flew. A bullet struck Rose in the upper part of the arm, close to Angela's head. In a desperate effort to shield the other woman, Rose Nicholson was again shot, this time in the head.

At the same instant the driver of the police car slumped at the wheel but the car was already at a standstill. A uniformed policeman came running, yelling: "Stop that car!" but either no one heard or no one dared. He tried desperately to see the number, but failed. The green car swung round the corner long before nurses and porters came hurrying to the two wounded women and the wounded man.

Roger felt a jolt, as if from physical violence, when Baker told him what had happened, and for a few seconds his reaction was one of shock. But that soon passed, and his voice was almost casual as he asked: "Are they hurt badly?"

"The policewoman is. She's on her way to hospital for an emergency operation."

"And Mrs. Margerison?"

"She's unconscious apparently from a wound in the temple but they don't think its fatal. The driver of the police car has a bullet wound in the left shoulder." Baker, too, was very matter-of-fact. "The gunman was a passenger in a green Morris Minor, driven by a woman. The car was ditched in a car park two miles away — we've no idea where the couple are."

"Description?" asked Roger.

"Very vague. The man's face was hidden by a peaked cap, the woman's by a scarf round her head. We don't even know whether they were old or young. The car's being tested for prints but so far there isn't a sign of one."

"There wouldn't be," said Roger bitterly.

After a pause, Baker asked. "What's on, Handsome?"

"We're getting close to the Bullion Boys," Roger told him.

"My God, are we!" Baker seemed to draw a deep breath. "Well, if they're as deadly as this, we want 'em, quick."

"You can be absolutely sure of one thing," Roger said. "They're deadly all right." As he rang off, he thought of Margerison's body which he had seen at Wapping headquarters of the Thames Division; and he thought of the man buried in the garden at 17, Lyon Avenue; and he thought of this attempt to kill Margerison's wife. That could only be to prevent her from talking. Another thought began to creep about in his mind, one he didn't like at all. He was staring at the three telephones as he pondered. The truth was that aftet the months in the wilderness, as it were, the Bullion Case had drawn him into its heart too quickly. He simply hadn't had time to think, and he must make time, not only to think, but to talk.

Appleby would be the very man.

Roger gave a faint smile at the coincidence that Appleby's wife was away at the same time as his; they would be two grass widowers. But the smile soon faded. When so many different things happened almost simultaneously, there was a danger of seeing them spilling over into one another; of not seeing the wood for the trees; of getting one's priorities wrong. And he couldn't afford to do this. That wasn't simply because he wanted to make amends for his misjudgement in the case; it was because the Bullion Boys were now proved to be cold-blooded and deadly. From being simply a daring robbery which had captured the public's admiration, it had become a threat to anyone who might be able to betray the perpetrators to the police.

Who, besides Angela Margerison, was in danger?

Who, besides Rose Nicholson, might be gravely injured, if not killed, as the men who had moved from 17, Lyon Avenue protected themselves?

What *were* the priorities?

The first thing, he decided, was that the Press should give the matter publicity. But before he could let them have the story he would have to get Coppell's approval.

Or — should he break the story, and face the Commander with a *fait accompli*?

He made a swift decision, and dialled Coppell's number.

7

EVIDENCE

"COMMANDER speaking." For once, Coppell wasn't protected by his secretary. Over the telephone his voice sounded very deep and hard.

"West here, sir."

"Haven't you had enough of me today?" asked Coppell with heavy humour.

"I've had enough of nearly everything today," Roger said. "Including murder."

Coppell asked sharply: "Who's dead now?"

In tense sentences, Roger told him about the attack on the police car, and its consequences. Coppell was so long replying that Roger wondered if he had been cut off. Slowly, the familiar heavy breathing sounded, he was still there and no doubt fighting for composure. There was a tap at Roger's door and he covered the mouthpiece and called "Come in." The door opened to admit a rather sheepish, and awkward-moving Venables. Roger shooed him away and he closed the door with extreme caution.

"What do you want to do?" Coppell asked at last.

"Give the whole story to the newspapers."

"Why?"

"We need help from the public about the shooting tonight. Someone might come forward, especially if television or one of the newspapers plays up the human side: a criminal murdered, his devoted wife attacked —"

"All right, I'll buy that," Coppell interrupted. "What else?"

"We might pick up someone who passed along Lyon Avenue by night, or regularly by day but isn't within the reach of a door-to-door call," Roger added.

There was another pause before Coppell grunted: "Okay. Go ahead."

"Won't you do it, sir?"

"What? A Press conference?"

"Yes."

There was yet another pause, before Coppell answered: "No. It's your job. If you win you win, if you lose you lose. The eyes of the nation are upon you. Not to mention the reputation of the Yard."

He rang off, abruptly.

Roger thought: "What the devil *is* needling him?"

Coppell's attitude was puzzling, a curious mixture of antagonism and co-operation. Perhaps the explanation was as simple as he had said: he wanted Roger to take the kicks if this failed but was prepared to give him the kudos if the use of the newspapers succeeded. The main thing was that he agreed about giving the whole story to the Press, in fact all the news media. Roger picked up his inter-office telephone and dialled the Back Room. A man answered in a voice which sounded testy; a fed-up voice with a marked Scottish accent.

"Who is it now?"

"Superintendent West, Eric. I — "

"Thank the Lord for small mercies," exploded Eric McFee, recently appointed the chief inspector in charge of liaison with the Press. "I've a howling mob down here demanding a story about the shooting, and the telephones never stop. Can you come down and quieten the mob, somehow?" From the way he talked it was obvious that his room was crowded with newspapermen, who would be able to overhear and be ready to enter into the spirit of his plaints.

"Yes," Roger said. "Right away."

"The Lord be praised. Did you hear that? Superintendent West is coming down in person to the lions' den." McFee rang off, Roger smiled and stood up — and before he was halfway across the room there was a tap at the door. He called "Come in," and opened it at the same time, to an embarrassed Venables, whose hand was raised for another tap. He backed into the path of a superintendent, who gave him a sour look.

"I'm sorry, sir," Venables mumbled to him. And in a more earnest tone he went on to Roger: "I am *very* sorry, sir."

"What do you want?" asked Roger.

"I've just come back from the laboratory, sir, with some reports, but if this is still a bad time — "

"You'd better come with me and talk as we go," Roger said. "I'm going to the Back Room."

Venables moved diffidently towards the lifts; but once he began reporting, he was completely self-assured.

"I've my own written report on what

happened up to the time I left 17, Lyon Avenue," he stated. "I'll put it on your desk, sir, for you to read at leisure. The laboratory staff over at Holborn tell me that you've had a verbal report on the glass, and they've promised a written confirmation first thing tomorrow morning. The dust and small oddments found at Number 17 are of no help at all. The polish used on the floorboards and certain tools was a popular make which can be bought at any shop or supermarket — nothing from that, sir. The dirt itself is normal household dust, with some face powder found mixed with it in two bedrooms — again, a very popular make which can be bought at Woolworth's and almost any supermarket or chemist. One piece of a fingernail, a man's, was found and might conceivably be proved to have come from a particular hand — " He paused, glanced down at his feet, and sallied: "If we could only find the hand, sir."

The lift came up and the doors opened.

"Go on," Roger said, stepping inside.

"Not a single fingerprint of any kind anywhere, inside or out," Venables went on gloomily.

"Who told you that?"

"Division, sir. And *Fingerprints* here. All the garden tools we hadn't touched were brought here for testing."

"Go on," Roger urged again, as they began to ascend.

"There were two or three heelmarks in the garden — on freshly dug beds — and plaster casts have been taken of these. Division will send them over, sir. They're all of a woman's heels. And except for two things you may have been told about, that's all."

"What are those two things?"

"They found two shavings of gold, sir."

"Yes, Green told me," Roger said, reflecting that this at least was good. "Any test been made on them yet?"

"No, sir — they were sent over to the Bank of England for identification, and we won't know for a few hours. I couldn't get any promise out of the people there, sir."

"That doesn't surprise me," Roger said. "And the final thing?"

"The machine fastened to the floor was a pretty heavy one," answered Venables. "It was stuck down, as we know, to the tiles with a very powerful industrial adhesive.

Under close inspection all the tiles on which it stood proved to have a myriad of tiny cracks. So the machine must have been fairly weighty."

"And it would take some moving," Roger said, slowly.

"Unless it was taken in part by part and assembled on the spot, sir, and then taken to pieces to get it out of the house," Venables pointed out.

Roger's heart began to beat fast, and he stopped in the passage a few yards away from the Back Room which, in the new building, was in the front despite the use of the old name. Venables *was* good. And he no doubt saw what this meant: that if the machine had been assembled and reassembled, the job had to be done by an expert: probably a qualified engineer.

"So we want a man used to putting a lathe together and taking it apart again," Roger said.

Venables' eyes lit up.

"We do, sir! Er — shall I wait in your office, or have you finished with me tonight?"

"Come in here with me," Roger decided. "I can bring you up to date with what's going on while I'm talking to the others."

He opened the door of the Back Room, and a subdued rumble of voices sounded, from twenty-five to thirty men crowded into a room with only twenty upright, metal chairs. Several stood at the sides, three of these with ordinary cameras, one with a camera already on a tripod: almost certainly a television unit. In a desk behind the door, tall, dark-haired, dark-eyed Eric McFee stood talking to a much shorter man. When he saw Roger he raised his hand in welcome and the others in the room obviously took this for a signal, and near-silence fell. McFee, who looked more Cornish than Scottish, with jutting eyebrows making his eyes seem more deep-set than they were, placed a hand on the other's shoulder, and called:

"Glad to see you, Superintendent. I've told them you'll probably want to make a statement first, and then answer questions, it's all yours."

"That's right," Roger said. He was aware of several men looking curiously at Venables. There had been no time to marshal his thoughts on the way here because of listening to Venables, and his mind seethed with the information the Sergeant had brought. But as he sat on a corner of McFee's desk, and surveyed the faces of the newspapermen, what he had to say seemed to drop into his mind. As he talked, he observed: half of these men were in their fifties, old, experienced crime reporters on the national Press. Some looked like boys. There was one woman, middle-aged and grey-haired.

A man at the side called: "Is it the Bullion Case, Mr. West?"

Roger answered promptly: "Yes."

"My God!" someone else called. "You were right, Tab."

"Is it certain?" a man with an American or Canadian accent called out.

"Positive," Roger said, hesitated, and went on: "You're all in time to catch the morning editions, aren't you?"

There was a chorus of "Yes" but two men waved to attract attention and the one at the camera on the tripod pleaded:

"I need to be out in half an hour if I'm to catch the main news."

"Same here," another man called.

"I won't need half an hour," Roger said. "I've a lot to do. So let me give you the salient facts." He raised a finger. "*One*. The van driver involved in the Bullion Robbery, David Margerison, was found dead, in the Thames this morning. He didn't die from drowning, but the autopsy report isn't in yet so we don't know exactly how he did die. *Two*. An attempt was made to murder his wife/widow when she was being taken in a police car to the Marley Nursing Home, Marley Street, this afternoon."

Someone called: "Half a moment, please." Nearly every head was bent, nearly every hand was moving with pen or pencil over notepad or scraps of old envelopes. Roger waited until most heads were lifted, and went on.

"*Three*. A man and a woman in a green Morris Minor number JLT 5123 were involved in the shooting. The abandoned car was found in a car park at Islington, the driver and the gunman having escaped. We are particularly anxious to hear from anyone who saw them leave the car, and the means of their getaway. We have no useful descriptions yet. *Four*. We now know that the Bullion Boys holed up at 17, Lyon Avenue, Chiswick, and we are nearly sure they melted down a lot of the gold there. Neighbours say that they were night-workers, and we want anyone who used that part of Chiswick by night to come forward with any information they can give us. Night or day, for that matter."

Again, a man pleaded: "Half a mo'."

Another called: "Can you be more precise about 'used that part of Chiswick'?"

"Yes," answered Roger. "Night-workers from restaurants, musicians, the staff and cast at theatres and cinemas almost certainly use Lyon Avenue on their way to and from work. It's not a main road but it feeds a big new housing estate from the Chiswick High Street and is extensively used. We need the descriptions of any men known to have gone in or out of that house — of cars, vans or lorries pulled up outside at night: in fact, anything which anyone noticed could be of vital importance."

Most heads were now raised; most lips seemed poised for questions, and the woman began to speak.

"Can you tell us more about Margerison's wife, Mr. West?"

"And the injured policewoman?" another called out.

Roger pursed his lips before saying very gravely: "*Five*. Angela Margerson came to the house obviously expecting to see her husband, just after we reached the place. That's how we came to interview her. She had been meeting him there every week. I had to tell her that her husband was dead." He paused, with unconscious dramatic effect, and then went on: "She collapsed, and went into a state of shock. She was on the way to the nursing home for special care when the attack was made. Police Constable Rose Nicholson was wounded while trying to protect Mrs. Margerison from bullets. Obviously, the attackers fear that she can give us information vital to them."

He stopped.

"If they've tried once they may try again," a man suggested.

"Obviously."

"So special precautions should be taken at the nursing home."

"They are being taken."

"May we know what they are?" the first speaker asked.

"No," Roger answered. "Secret precautions are by far the best."

Someone chuckled. The woman in the corner asked:

"How *is* Mrs. Margerison?"

"I've nothing to say except that she is having special care. Obviously it's better for the assailants not to know what that care is."

No one argued, but the woman asked: "How is Policewoman Nicholson?"

"Very seriously injured indeed."

"At death's door?"

"So I understand," Roger answered heavily.

There was a brief hiatus in the proceedings, and Roger wondered if the newspapermen had all they needed, when a small man from the *Daily Globe* called out:

"Did you find any gold there, Mr. West? At Lyon Avenue, I mean."

"A few filings," Roger answered.

"Do you know how long the Bullion Boys had been there?"

"As far as we can judge, six months."

"And Margerison's wife went there every week?"

"After the first few weeks, yes."

"Wasn't she watched by the police?"

the same man asked, and Roger's heart gave a lurch.

"For those first few weeks, yes."

"And afterwards?"

"The surveillance was discontinued," Roger said flatly. "On my instructions."

At first, few of the reporters had realised where this was leading to, but at this juncture everyone seemed to go stiff and alert. Tension had suddenly come in place of a relaxed and friendly atmosphere. Venables moistened his lips and stood at his full height. McFee clenched his fists, aggressive in his unspoken defence of Roger.

Then the man who had asked this series of questions put one which was inevitable even though the phrasing of it came like a hammer blow.

"In that case, Mr. West, wouldn't it be true to say that these murders, and the attack on the policewoman as well as on Margerison's wife were directly due to your earlier course of action?"

8

PRESS CHALLENGE

THERE was utter silence after the questioner's voice stopped; and no one moved. Into the silence came a whisper, words spoken in a tone which could not usually have been heard but were carried on the silence and by the acoustics of the room.

"That's bloody unfair."

It was Venables — and on that instant, practically every eye in the room was turned towards him. At first, obviously, he did not realise that everyone had heard. As realisation dawned on him, he turned a dusky red. Yet he also squared his shoulders and looked into the crowd of faces; and as if in a defiance born out of the situation, he said:

"Well, it *is* bloody unfair."

McFee leaned closer to Roger.

"Who's that, Handsome?"

The questioner was one of the few men who concentrated on Roger, not on the young detective officer, and he asked very clearly:

"This isn't a personal issue, Superintendent, I have the greatest respect for you. As I'm sure everyone present has. But in this particular case, isn't it true that an error of judgement on the part of the police led directly to these new crimes?" Before Roger could frame a reply, and as a single subdued: "*Shame!*" came from someone near the door, the questioner went on: "And isn't it also true that the same error of judgement led to the failure of the police to find not only the thieves known commonly as the Bullion Boys, but also a substantial quantity of the stolen gold?"

As he finished speaking, the man stood up. It was Samuel Gaddison, the *Daily Globe*'s best man; one of London's keenest newspapermen. He was small and undistinguished looking, with greying hair and a bald patch. The collar of his jacket was turned up, everything about him looked careless; only his phraseology was sharp and immaculate. Obviously he wanted it to be seen and known that it was he who was putting the question.

As he finished, everyone's gaze was turned towards Roger.

It was never wise to judge from appearances, but he did not sense a great deal of sympathy here. The questions were factual; these were men who dealt in facts, and they would be swift to pounce on any evasion or half-truth. Roger thought wryly: Coppell may have anticipated something like this and made sure he didn't run into it.

From the thick of the seated men came a demand: "*Answer*".

"Oh, I'll answer," Roger said confidently enough. His heart was thumping and his whole body felt cold. "And of course it's a question — they are all questions — which I've asked myself. Obviously, the basic implication is right: an error was made, and the consequences so far have been disastrous. I could argue that if we'd kept a constant watch on Angela Margerison she might never have been allowed to visit her husband and so we would never have linked her with the house. I could also say that sooner or later she might have gone to see him and had we still been watching her carefully enough, we could have caught him." He raised his hands in a helpless kind of gesture, and went on: "But it isn't quite as simple as that."

"I should have thought it was just as simple as that," interjected Gaddison. "An error was made, and the result was disastrous."

"Well, obviously you can look at it that way," Roger conceded. "And I shan't complain if you do. I'm much more concerned with what my superiors at the Yard think. But whatever you say, I hope you'll get your facts absolutely right. This was not an oversight. It was not an error of omission, something I would have done had I thought of it. It was a deliberately calculated risk. If I had to face the same situation again, in the same circumstances, I think I would take the same risk."

"I would have thought that made the situation worse," interpolated Gaddison again, his voice quiet and convincing. "A calculated error is surely worse than an oversight."

"I don't think so," Roger retorted. "I had a choice — "

"You know, Superintendent," McFee interrupted, "you don't have to subject yourself to this cross-examination."

"Hear, hear!" exclaimed Venables, as if words had been bursting to force their way between his lips.

Someone called: "Don't back down now, Handsome."

Roger smiled. He was surprised by his own calmness; this was nothing like the effort he had expected it to be, and awareness of the reactions which would set in afterwards was very hazy on his mind.

"I think the situation ought to be explored," he declared. "I don't think there is anyone present, least of all Mr. Gaddison, who would deliberately misinterpret things said, or deliberately distort situations. But if they don't fully understand, then they could mislead and distort out of sheer ignorance of the facts." He paused long enough to acknowledge a smile which came from Gaddison, and went on: "I was saying that I had a choice of action. I could either deploy at least two or better still four men to keep a day and night watch on Mrs. Margerison, since she was our only possible lead. However, the Bullion Robbery was not the only case preoccupying me or the Yard at the time."

For the first time he saw a slackening of

tension in some of the faces, and out of the corner of his eye he saw Venables wipe his forehead with a big, very white handkerchief.

"Some of you may remember the acid-throwing troubles we had. Young lovers in the parks and on the commons were sprayed with sulphuric acid. We ran into that investigation about five weeks after the Bullion Robbery, and it took a lot of time and a lot of men to solve it. Somehow we never have quite enough men to do everything. I took those who were watching Mrs. Margerison off and assigned them to jobs which seemed at the time more urgent and important. That's what I think I would have to do in similar circumstances again. But whether four less men would have prevented us from solving the acid-throwing case, whether they were essential on that job, I really don't know."

He stopped, then asked clearly: "Are there any more questions?"

"Yes," called Gaddison, "are you saying that the basic cause of what happened today is that the C.I.D. is understaffed?"

Roger hesitated for a long time, but no one interrupted and no one left the room.

He was more than ever anxious not to appear to be offering an excuse, but these questions had done him good, for they had made him think more about the whole situation; it *was* true that he had taken the watch off Angela Margerison because there weren't enough men to go round. On the other hand he could have left the men on; or he could have put them back after the acid-throwing emergency.

"No," he said at last. "I think I would have kept her under surveillance if we had more staff, but I had a choice to make, a free choice. And the one I made has led to the present situation. Now!" He squared his shoulders and looked about the room. "Are there any more questions?"

None was put, but suddenly someone clapped, and others joined in; and before the conference broke up, they were nearly all clapping. McFee actually joined in. Roger saw with amusement that Venables had thrust his hands deep in his trouser pockets, as if to make sure he didn't take part. Gaddison came over, pushing through the crowd.

"That really wasn't meant to get at you personally," he said.

"I'm sure it wasn't," Roger replied. "On the other hand it couldn't miss me, could it?" He shrugged, and went on: "I've had a very good run in the Press generally, although I've got into trouble once or twice lately."

"No hard feelings?" Gaddison asked hopefully.

"No hard feelings," Roger assured him, and added quickly: "Until I've seen tomorrow's *Globe*, anyhow!"

There was a general laugh.

When he left the office with Venables just behind him, Roger felt both tired and relaxed. The lights were on, now; he hadn't realised how dark or how late it was; after six o'clock certainly. In an hour, he ought to be at Appleby's place. He reached his own office, with Venables at his side.

"Are you in a particular rush to get home?"

"No, sir!" Venables could not be emphatic enough.

"You check with the laboratory about the splinter of glass," Roger said. "Chief Inspector Smythe told me there is only one manufacturer and only a few places where that particular glass is used, and he was going to send the list. If he's got it, make a schedule for visiting each place, will you?"

"By car or train?" asked Venables.

"Road, train or air," Roger said. "Whichever seems most practicable."

"I'll do that, sir — and shall I bring the schedule out to your house?"

Roger pursed his lips. Venables was obviously eager; was he by any chance too eager? Did he see this as a heaven-sent chance to visit Roger at home? Hurriedly, he went on:

"It would be very easy, sir — I live at Putney, and could drop it in as I pass. And could leave the general report at the same time."

"Good idea." Roger decided that there was no point in pouring cold water on enthusiasm, unless it threatened to cause embarrassment or problems. "If I'm not there, one of my sons probably will be." He added in a burst of communicativeness: "I shall be dining with Dr. Appleby who should have both post-mortem reports ready by the time I reach his home."

Venables stood very upright, with an expression on his face it was difficult to understand. Then he said hesitatingly:

"You really never stop, sir, do you?"

"There's a lot to do," Roger dissembled.

"Yes, sir — too much, if you ask me. May I say how much I admired the way you conducted the conference tonight? It was — it was *masterly*. Good-night, sir!" Obviously embarrassed by his own outburst, he turned and hurried along the passage. It was astonishing how quickly and silently he moved. He didn't look back, and Roger went across to his desk, switching on a desk-lamp. There were several messages, none of them of any consequence; no matter what case was demanding most attention, the routine matters went on.

He had to have a medical check next month.

He hadn't paid for his tickets to the South Western dinner-dance.

He had promised to present the prizes at a Charity Sports Night, two weeks from now. He sent a cheque, confirmed the prize-giving by telephone, and at six-thirty started down to collect his own car from the garage beneath the new building. It was strange how empty the place seemed, and yet how busy *information* was, with the uniformed men sitting at their teletype machines and the messages being taken along on a kind of conveyor. Even in his time at the Yard the degree of modernisation had been remarkable. Often, police cars were at the scene within two minutes of a crime having been reported.

He opened the door opposite the lift hall, and the inspector on duty looked up.

"Good-evening, sir."

"Anything new for me?" asked Roger.

"It depends on what you call new, sir," the Chief Inspector said. He looked so young: thirty or so, and he made Roger, in his mid-forties, feel old. "Nothing since the report on the death of Police Officer Rose Nicholson, sir."

Roger gave an involuntary start. His expression must have changed so much and the shock been so obvious that the other man moved quickly towards him. Roger's mouth went suddenly dry. All about him were the men tap-tap-tapping at their machines, a buzz of sound, a constant undertone of voices as men talked on the telephone; and the long windows with the conveyor passing message after message to Information Control.

"Didn't you get the message, sir?" the Chief Inspector asked, helplessly.

"No," Roger muttered. "No. When did she die?"

"I sent the message along to your office by hand, sir, as there was no reply when I called you. I didn't want to disturb you in the Back Room."

"No," Roger repeated. "Quite right. I — I shall be all right. It was a shock. I feel that I — " He broke off, and moistened his lips and wished above all things for a nip of whisky or brandy. Good God, this news had shaken him! But there was no use telling this man that he felt he had sent the woman to her death. He had worn sackcloth and ashes more than enough today. What the hell was making him feel so sensitive? He looked at his watch, and went on: "I'd better call the Back Room," and went across to the Chief Inspector's desk and dialled McFee, who answered while talking to someone else.

"Well, I'd say it was a bloody good show and if any crummy newspaper crucifies Handsome for it their man had better not show up here again — who's that?"

"West," said Roger drily.

"Who? I — Hallo, sir," boomed McFee, pretending that he did not know Roger must have heard what he said: "Best impromptu conference we've had since — "

"Have you been told that Rose Nicholson's dead?" demanded Roger.

There was a sharp sound and an intake of breath before McFee said in a very different tone: "No sir, I didn't know."

"I've just been told. We need to make a formal statement — with her age, rank, years of service, everything that matters. And her family needs telling before the news gets out." In a heavy voice, Roger went on: "I'd better go and see them."

"I can tell you this, sir," McFee said. "She's a married woman living apart from her husband. She has no relatives in London but an elderly aunt and uncle in Suffolk — I checked so as to put out a statement earlier. So that's one nasty job you don't have to do."

Roger said with relief: "All right, if you're sure." He put down the receiver and studied the face of the *Information* man, who was obviously in deep concern. He made himself say: "And that's the lot?"

"Yes, sir."

"If I'm wanted tonight I'll be at Dr. Appleby's place in St. John's Wood."

"Would you care for a car, sir?"

"No," Roger said roughly. "I'm all right. I don't need — " He broke off, seeing the change in the other's expression, and then forced a laugh. "Yes, I *will* have a car," he decided. "I'll be in the courtyard in a few minutes, waiting for it." He went off, and along to the lifts and down to the ground floor; and everywhere he went he seemed to see Rose Nicholson's face, with its compassion and concern. He drew in a deep breath as he stepped out into the chill night air and muttered to himself: "It's going to take a hell of a time to get over this case."

Then a car pulled up, a police driver at the wheel. He climbed into it, and closed his eyes.

9

DAN APPLEBY

THE house where Daniel Appleby lived had the look of having been there forever. In fact it was less than a hundred years old, but the once-yellow brick had weathered to brown, helped by the smuts and smoke before the heart of London had been made a smokeless zone. High above one side rose a huge apartment block. On the other was a smaller apartment block, with yet another just behind. The house itself was one of six, all that were left of St. John's Wood's yesterdays.

The entrance hall had been freshly painted a pale green. The odour of paint was very strong. The stairs of stone had a strip of haircord carpet down the middle. There was no lift. Roger went up to the third floor, and approached Flat 5, which was still awaiting its coat of paint, the ladder and dust sheets stored on the half-landing above. Roger rang a bell in the centre of the door panel, and the ringing sound was harsh and over-loud. He half-expected Dot Appleby to open the door, cigarette in one hand and gin in the other.

But it was Appleby, in a blue velveteen smoking-jacket which hung loosely on his knobbly frame. He looked a boy. His fair, downy hair might have been that of a teenager, while his eyebrows and eyelashes, much darker than his hair, gave him an expression of permanent surprise; or was it enquiry?

"C-come in, Handsome." He shook hands and closed the door. "You l-l-look as if you could do with a s-s-snort." He led the way in to a finely proportioned room, which had a somewhat dilapidated appearance, the furniture having aged more quickly than Appleby appeared to have done. On either wall at the fireplace were bookshelves crammed to overflowing, books upright, books on their sides, books at all angles and of all shapes and sizes. The fireplace was huge, but instead of coal or wood or smokeless fuel, an electric fire glowed a lack-lustre red.

On a side table were bottles, glasses, openers and a bowl of ice.

"What will you have?" Appleby asked.

"Whisky and soda, if I may."

"I'll join you." Appleby poured out and brought Roger's glass across. "Cheers," he toasted. "And perdition to the Bullion Boys!"

"Now that's what I want to drink to." Roger sipped, fighting back a temptation to gulp the whole drink down as he lowered himself to one of the big shabby chairs, and stretched his legs out. "How's Dot?" he asked.

Appleby was standing in front of him, looking down quizzically.

"D-d-dear, d-d-darling Dot is d-d-divorcing me," he stated clearly.

Roger sat up suddenly, whisky spilling over the side of his glass.

"Good God!"

"B-bit of a shock, isn't it?" Appleby remarked, calmly. "Here, let me." He took a handkerchief out of his pocket and dabbed at the dark stains on Roger's sleeve. "Well, that's l-l-life. I saw her this afternoon. That's why I was late with the Margerison autopsy. It's absolutely final." He drank again, and his manner had changed, his stammer had deserted him: it often did when he was concentrating.

"And a damned good thing," he added. After a pause he relaxed, gave a rather wry smile, and asked: "Shocked?"

"No," Roger said. "I hadn't been expecting it, though."

"No one had."

"Dan," Roger said. "I'm glad."

"Straight from the onlooker's mouth," said Appleby.

"If you'd rather I didn't talk about it — " began Roger.

"T-t-talk as much as you l-like, old b-b-boy! I need strength and support to justify myself. We were not truly suited, were we?"

"No."

"And gin didn't help, you know."

"Ah," said Roger. "I thought so."

"And while I am no psychiatrist, even a pathologist with his knives knows that when an attractive and intelligent woman really takes to drink she isn't the happiest woman in the world."

"Is there someone else?"

"Nope!" exclaimed Appleby. "With neither of us. Sad truth is that we grew to hate the sight of each other. And whatever else you may say of the new divorce laws, they make it possible to get a divorce without a lot of lying and pretending. So — she has been to her solicitors. I have been to mine. Twenty years ended, so to speak." He drained his glass, and stared out of the window, his expression empty of all emotion. "It was a mistake from the start. I knew it within months. Weeks. Sometimes I wonder what makes human beings go on living, lying, pretending to love while wallowing in hate." He gave a harsh bark of a laugh. "Man's inhumanity to women, and vice versa. You never have that kind of problem, do you, Handsome?"

After a pause, Roger said: "Not in the same way." When Appleby didn't look round, he went on: "Do you really want to talk about it?"

"About D-D-Dot and me?" At last, Appleby turned round. "No, Handsome. Not really t-t-talk. I did want a man's company tonight, a man I liked, to whom I could t-t-tell the simple facts without having t-t-to wallow in self-pity or self-reproach. However, I may have lopped off an arm, so to speak, no longer of use to me, but the lopping hurt and the wound is raw. If I'm a l-l-little difficult tonight, be understanding. I have a casserole in the oven. I am a very g-g-good cook. I have been the b-b-best and often the only c-c-cook in this household for years. Ready to eat?"

They were both ready.

It was a beefsteak casserole, and delicious. There was fruit, cream and ice cream to follow. When they had finished in the little dining room, Appleby insisted on leaving everything as it was.

"I've a good d-d-daily," he claimed. "Now c-c-coffee and brandy and c-c-corpus findings!"

There was something almost macabre in the way he could talk about his job; the dissecting of a human body. But there was a clinical clarity, too, and a picture of a live man, and a dead one formed gradually in Roger's mind. Margerison had been in robust health and physical fitness; a man of about forty, unusually handsome, very sound teeth with two gold fillings, dark hair inclined to curl, grey eyes . . .

"How did he die?" asked Roger.

"He was first dosed with a barbiturate and then dumped in the river. Barbiturate poisoning caused death. I've most of the report ready, you can have it tomorrow. I would p-p-put the date of d-d-death as possibly a week ago. I c-c-can't get any closer on the actual time. He made no struggle, of that I'm sure. Now! The second man was also dosed with a barbiturate. I would say he was killed a day or so more recently. The body was naked; identification m-m-might be made by the dentist who put a g-g-gold filling in his left side molar about a year ago."

Appleby broke off, obviously because Roger was staring so intently. Roger's heart was beating very fast, now, with the kind of excitement which often came when it looked as if a case were beginning to break.

"Do you know which barbiturate?"

"I would say one of the Nembutal group. They are easy t-t-to get as painkillers, Handsome."

Roger said bitterly: "First kill the senses, then kill — " he broke off.

"Feel strongly?" Appleby asked, as if surprised.

"Didn't you hear about the death of the policewoman?"

"Oh, God. No." Appleby seemed shaken "How?"

"She was shot during an attempt to kill Margerison's wife," Roger told him.

"Oh, God," groaned Appleby again. "Worse and worse."

"Could there be any doubt about the barbiturate?"

"None."

"May I use the telephone?" Roger asked, and as Appleby nodded he moved across to a fireside table, and dialled the Holborn number of the Forensic Science Laboratory, and almost at once a woman answered; that would be one of the women laboratory assistants. "Good-evening," Roger said. "This is Superintendent West."

"Good-evening, sir."

"That dust which was taken from 17, Lyon Avenue — "

"I've just been looking at the reports and analysis," the laboratory woman said.

"Can you check quickly to see if there's any indication of barbiturates in any form?" Roger asked.

"I will, yes."

"Call me back at Dr. Appleby's, will you?"

"In about an hour," the woman promised.

Appleby was pouring out some coffee; he listened intently to the whole story of the splinter of glass, and before Roger asked, volunteered:

"This blue shading is probably a trade mark, made by a special kind of transfer until it's almost part of the glass. You sure it is blue?"

"A pale — well, a light rather than a dark blue. Do you know anybody who uses a blue trade mark?"

Appleby nodded, quite calmly.

"There's one big company, K & K," he replied thoughtfully. "They might be your b-b-best b-b-bet, for a start. They're in S-S-Staffordshire, not far from Stone. I know the managing director up there, he's m-m-most helpful. M-m-man named Crabb. And I've an idea that if they didn't actually make whatever your splinter came from, they're likely to know who did. They've a very strong research department. W-w-would it help if I c-c-called him?"

"Now?"

"Why not?"

Roger said: "Fine, thanks," and Appleby stretched out his hand and then pulled it away again for the bell rang before he touched it. He laughed, then lifted the receiver.

"Ap-Ap-Appleby... Who?...? Why, yes, he's here. H-h-hold on half a mo'. C-c-could you come round for a d-d-drink ...? Good ...! Fifteen minutes, then. Want to speak to him now? Okay!" Appleby put the receiver down, and beamed across at Roger. "Fitzpatrick," he announced. "He says he wants to talk to you about Margerison's wife. He only lives at Swiss Cottage. Then you'll have all your expert opinion, won't you? Shall I still call Crabb?"

Roger said, "Yes, please. And I'll talk to him when you've done."

Appleby plucked up the receiver and opened a telephone-list, beginning to dial almost at once. He sat back, looking more relaxed than at any time this evening, and Roger watched him, wondering how he really felt about the impending divorce. He had a dozen flash thoughts: about the splinter of glass and the gold filings and the lab report which Venables had collected.

"Wally Crabb?" Appleby said into the telephone. "Dan Appleby . . . Fine, thanks, and a friend of mine needs s-s-some help. A very d-d-distinguished friend at Scotland Yard . . . Handsome West . . . So you've heard of him! Who hasn't! Here he is."

Roger took the receiver from a large but very well shaped hand.

"Mr. Crabb . . ."

"Very interested to hear I can help you," Crabb said. He had a voice with a faint overtone of the North Country, deep and friendly. "And of course I'll be glad to."

"I want to try to identify the nature and source of a splinter of glass," Roger stated. "Does that sound possible?"

"It sounds like a tall order, but why don't we have a look at it?" asked Crabb. "How soon do you want to know? Tonight, I suppose!"

"Is that possible?" asked Roger.

"We could try. We've a night shift at the factory and if our chief chemist isn't there then we can soon get him. Shall I lay it on?"

Roger hesitated for a few moments before answering in a reasoned voice:

"I think I'll wait until nine o'clock in the morning, if that's all right with you."

"To tell you the truth it's much better," Crabb said. "We can really pull out all the stops then. Will you come by road?"

"Yes."

"Come from Stafford to the Stone roundabout," advised Crabb. "I'll have one of our vans with K & K very large and clear. The driver will lead you to the factory, which can be difficult to find."

"You're very good," Roger said appreciatively.

"Very glad to help a friend of Dan Appleby," said Crabb, and added with a laugh: "And the Yard, of course! I'll look forward to seeing you."

He rang off.

Roger put the receiver down and gave a laugh which was part rueful, part genuine amusement. He took a cup of coffee which Appleby was holding out, and sipped.

"Thanks. Well, he's a go-getter!"

"Wally Crabb?" asked Appleby, smiling.

"Yes. A couple of dozen more like him in British industry and we wouldn't have an economic crisis. He — but judge for yourself when you see him."

Five minutes later there was a ring at the front door bell, and Appleby let Dr.

Michael Fitzpatrick in. Fitzpatrick was a short, rotund, pink-and-white person, but his plump hand had an unexpectedly firm grip. He accepted a whisky and soda, and they talked idly for a few moments, although none of them had a bent for small talk. Soon, Fitzpatrick turned to look intently at Roger.

"The Margerison woman," he said.

"How is she?" asked Roger, more tensely than he had expected.

"She is in a state of shock, and you don't need a psychiatrist to tell you that." Fitzpatrick sat back in his chair. "The glancing wound on her temple isn't serious, and certainly not the cause of the coma."

"Coma?"

"Undoubtedly a coma," stated Fitzpatrick.

"How long will she be in it?" Roger asked.

"It could be a day, a week or a month," Fitzpatrick answered. "It's no use beating about the bush, Handsome: so far as your immediate enquiries are concerned you may as well forget her. I can't tell you much about the state of her mind but I can tell you that this kind of nervous or mental collapse seldom comes without a long period of strain preceding it. Any attempt to jolt her out of the collapse — and it could be done with electric shock waves and drugs — could very well do a great deal of long term harm. I wouldn't consent to it. I'm sorry, but so far as she is concerned, you're on your own."

It was Appleby who said: "So all you've got, Handsome, is a splinter of glass."

10

ATTACK

ROGER said: "Yes, a splinter of glass," and for the first time wished he were at home, for Fitzpatrick was a fly fisherman and Appleby had an interest in the sport, and both became absorbed in talk of tackle and flies and trout and favourite spots in favourite streams. He was glad when the telephone bell rang, and answered it while the others lowered their voices. It was the woman from the laboratory.

"There *is* a little, a very little trace of Nembutal, Mr. West," she said. "But it could well have been there for years. When a tablet is dropped a small piece often breaks off and it's virtually indestructible."

"But it's undoubtedly a barbiturate in the Nembutal class?" Roger insisted.

"Yes, sir. But we haven't had much luck with the splinter of glass except that the blue marking looks like a trade mark."

"I'm going up to see a firm of glass manufacturers known as K & K in the morning," Roger said. "I'll take the splinter, and they may be able to help."

"I do hope they can," the woman answered, with obvious relief. "What time are you leaving, sir?"

"Early. You don't happen to know the address of P.C. Venables, who was in the lab earlier this evening, do you?"

The woman laughed.

"I have his address *and* telephone number, sir! He called an hour ago, with a query about one of the smaller glass manufacturers. Just one moment — "

When she came on the line again Roger asked her to have the splinter and some dust from 17, Lyon Avenue delivered to Venables' place, then asked for his telephone number. Soon he was dialling the number, and Venables himself answered.

"This is David Venables . . . Mr. West, sir!" It was easy to imagine that he turned a dusky red. "Yes, I've the schedule ready, sir, it's all a matter of timing and where you want to start your investigation."

"At K & K, in Staffordshire," Roger said.

"Road is best. It should take about three hours."

"Then we start from the Yard at six o'clock," Roger said, and promptly changed his mind. "Make it my house at six o'clock. Nothing new is likely at the Yard as early as that, and we'll keep in touch by radio-telephone. How will you get to my place?"

"By motor-cycle, sir."

A mental picture of Venables, looking rather like a Martian on the seat of a motor-cycle brought a curve to Roger's lips, but when he rang off he was smiling in an unexpectedly affectionate way; whatever the time and whatever the need, Venables was ready to work. He rang off, to the drone of Fitzpatrick's and Appleby's voices, still happily relating their fishing experiences.

"I hate to interrupt," Roger said, "but I ought to go, and before I do I'd be grateful for help."

"*You* want help!" scoffed Fitzpatrick.

"Have an-an-another spot before you go," Appleby offered.

"No, thanks," Roger refused. "I've come across a very promising youngster on the C.I.D. force who has a problem — you two can probably do more to help him than anyone. He was there when the body was dug up at Lyon Avenue, Dan, and the first whiff of decay nearly made him faint. He says he's often had this nausea. The sight of blood and injury doesn't worry him, but — "

"The odour of death does," Fitzpatrick said into a pause. "Is he just squeamish?"

"He's scared, in case it disqualifies him for the C.I.D.," said Roger. "What do you think, Dan?"

Appleby was pursing his lips.

"Well, I've known people who never got over it," he answered. "But most of them do if they have enough experience. I had a girl assistant once who fainted the first half-dozen times she saw a decayed body, but she stuck at it and was quite the best assistant I've ever had. I could give your chap some experience."

"I could probably find out if the cause lies in something which happened in his childhood," suggested Fitzpatrick. "And if it does, I could help him to overcome it. But Dan's way would probably be the quicker."

"Think he'd like to come to me for a

week or two?" asked Appleby. "We could soon find a way. I could ask for help of a man with certain qualifications, and you could recommend him. Is he really good?"

"I think he's going to be. And thanks, very much. I'll talk to him in the morning. Now I really must be off."

He took a cab to the Yard to fetch his own car, then drove himself back to Chelsea, and an empty house in a pleasant street, near the main road. There was a message signed by his two sons: *Don't wait up, Pop!* propped against an apple pie on the kitchen table. He went to bed, very thoughtfully. Janet was away because she urgently needed a rest from the routine of home life, of waiting for him day after day, never sure what time he would get back. A few weeks ago they had reached crisis point, but the crisis had been overcome in a mood of mutual understanding. All the same, there were times when he wondered whether they could really stay together happily unless he soon retired. He could retire almost any time, for he had already served for over twenty years in the Force, but he was well on the right side of fifty, and the Yard was his life. Of course, Janet might come back feeling very much better, and thank God there was nothing like the heavy drinking which had ruined Appleby's marriage.

He dropped off to sleep, his thoughts flitting from Janet to Dot Appleby, and from her to Rose Nicholson. There had been something about Rose which had attracted him. He hated the thought that any police officer had been killed because of his instructions, perhaps his misjudgement; and he hated it still more because something in her had seemed to respond to him. Compassion was one thing, but there had been some other quality. Her death hurt, his share of the responsibility for it hurt more: and it was no use soothing himself with the reminder that he had only known her for an hour or two.

In a clear, positive tone, he said to the dark room: "I'm going to get the devil who killed her."

Devil—

He dropped off to sleep only vaguely comprehending the fact that he wanted to avenge Rose Nicholson's murder at least as much as he wanted to catch the Bullion Boys.

The ringing of the alarm woke him; so it

was five-thirty. He felt heavy-eyed and tired, but made himself sit up. The only light was from a street-lamp, and the morning looked very dark, with neither moon nor stars. He got up, shaved quickly, and was downstairs at ten to six, time to make some toast — no, damn it, he'd eat that apple pie! He went into the kitchen, but there was no sign of the pie, except for an empty plate and two dirty forks in the sink. So Martin and Richard, his two sons, had wolfed his supper! He made coffee and toast, heard the pop-pop-pop of a motor-cycle and went into the front room. There in the road was Venables, looking huge and ungainly on a small motor-scooter, knees and feet at odd angles, a large white helmet obscuring his face. Why was it that he could never see or really think of this man without a smile?

He went out to the porch as Venables opened the gate. It was bitterly cold.

"Take my car out, and put the infernal machine into the garage," he said, handing over his keys. "Like some coffee?"

"No, thanks, sir. I'm fine."

"I'll be with you in a few moments." Roger went back, left a note for his boys, took a coat and his case, and let himself out. The car was parked at the kerb, and Venables was closing the garage doors.

"Will you drive, sir?"

"For a start," Roger said. "Wait until we're out of the centre of London before you begin reporting."

"Very good, sir."

Few people were about, and those mostly on bicycles. Here and there a uniformed policeman was on his beat, here and there one was testing a shop door. A few cars passed. The main street lights were on and they gave the West End a garish look. They went through Swiss Cottage and then out towards the M1, and were actually on the motorway before Roger told him about the barbiturate and all he had learned last night. Then:

"Anything new from your angle, Venables?"

"I got those dust and glass particles last night, sir. Apart from that and a few thoughts there's nothing new."

"What thoughts?" asked Roger.

Venables glanced at him and then stared straight ahead. A lot of traffic, headlights dipped, was already coming into London but not much was going out. Roger kept his gaze steadily on the road, noting the near-hypnotic pattern of the white lines before they disappeared beneath the wheels. At last, he said:

"I wondered whether we'd get any accurate descriptions of the man and woman in the green Morris Minor, sir, and whether we could get an Identikit picture done to take round to the people near 17, Lyon Avenue."

"We can fix that by telephone," Roger said.

"Yes, sir. Are we going to tell the newspapers how Mrs. Margerison is?"

Roger temporised: "What do you think?"

"I'd let them think she was doing well, sir — let them think that she is able to talk. And have her very closely guarded in case these killers tried again." He shot Roger another sideways, almost covert glance, and went on: "And I'd have her moved to a small place which could be strongly protected — and let the place where she is leak out. Unless you think that would be putting her in too much danger," Venables added hastily.

"As I placed Police Officer Nicholson, you mean?"

"Sir!" Venables said, and gulped before going on: "I thought that was wickedly unfair last night. You have to do things in the course of duty, and no one can be sure that everything will go well. But if you think it would be dangerous for Mrs. Margerison — "

"We'll think about it," Roger temporised. "Now let's see if the Yard has anything for us. We'll soon be out of range."

Venables flicked the radio-telephone on, and promptly *Information* answered. Venables said: "I'm speaking for Chief Superintendent West — "

Almost at once, a man with a Scottish accent began to talk.

"Good-morning, Mr. West . . . The request for information about the couple from the green Morris Minor is in all newspapers, sir, and in the popular ones on the front page . . . We have had seventeen telephone calls, in addition to a hundred and seven after the television news item last night. Having discounted the more eccentric ones, a certain amount of information, repeated too often not to be taken seriously, has emerged. It is this, sir: the couple separated near the nursing home, and the man got into a Ford van, plain grey, without any lettering, but it had a badly dented door panel. One of our men on patrol saw a girl picked up by a grey Ford van with a similar dent heading towards Brentford or Chiswick on the M4, sir. We have put a request out to Divisions for the grey van and the driver and passenger."

"Anything else?" Roger enquired.

"I heard you, sir," said the man at *Information*. "All reports say that the man had very black hair. There are a dozen variations in the description of the girl's hair and in any case she wore a scarf tied round her head. But the man appears to have lost his cap or hat, sir — at Marley Street he wore one, when he got out of the little car, he didn't."

"Thanks," Roger said, leaning closer to the mouthpiece which Venables held out. "See that I get reports along the motorway if they're urgent. Otherwise contact me through the Stone police, at the K & K factory."

"Right, sir"

Venables switched off.

Roger was pondering the very dark hair of the driver of the green Morris. Little if anything in this case was left to chance. The man might have lost his cap by accident but might just as well have taken it off deliberately to show his dark hair; which could have been dyed, to mislead the police. The more he thought, the more he puzzled about the attack on Angela Margerison and Rose Nicholson. It had been extremely daring, and so Angela must have some information they regarded as deadly. And clearly they would hesitate at nothing to protect themselves.

Where were they hiding?

In London? But where?

"My God!" he exclaimed.

"Sir?" asked Venables.

"They've had to move somewhere."

After a pause, Venables uttered: "Good God!" And after a moment of consternation he went on: "Shall I get *Information*?"

"Yes." Roger hesitated, looked in his mirror and saw several cars behind him and on the passing lane but none on the inside, so he pulled over and slowed down and finally stopped on the verge. By that time

Information was holding on, cars were swishing by, a big petrol delivery truck roared past. "*Information*," Roger said. "I want a check made, urgently, with estate agents, local councils and anyone else who might control property, to find out what houses or shop premises, even factory premises, have had new tenants in the past seven days. Furnished or unfurnished, and at least as roomy as 17, Lyon Avenue. Is that all clear?"

"All clear, sir — I'll put it in hand at once," the inspector in charge promised. "While you're on, there are two things for you. The number of reports about the dark-haired man and the girl getting out of the green Morris Minor and into the plain grey van has gone up to seventy-five. There is an unusual concensus of identification, sir. There is no report of the grey van yet, although one was seen at the Western end of the Great West Road, stopped at the traffic lights. We are trying to get more information."

"Right. What else?" asked Roger.

"It is South African gold, sir — that filing, I mean. An expert from South Africa House is sure it's from the Rand

Refinery in Germiston, near Johannesburg. It has the characteristic impurities, some silver, some copper, iron, lead and some stuff called palladium — like the music hall, sir! Apparently there's no difficulty in checking on a spectograph. The expert thinks it could be established whether it came off a bar in the particular shipment which was stolen."

"How can it be established?" demanded Roger.

"By sending it to Johannesburg — or rather Germiston, sir, where the Rand Refinery has special equipment to analyse the gold which may have the same impurities but in different proportions. It may also have other impurities in infinitesimal quantities but still measurable by spectographic analysis. The impurity and quantity vary slightly from mine to mine, and even vein to vein in the same mine."

Roger said, almost to himself: "Can we trust it to the post, I wonder?"

"There's no need, sir. Two South African C.I.D. men who came here to check on the I.D.B. case are going back this afternoon. They could take the sample."

"Give them half of what we've got, and tell them we'll be in their debt forever if they'll have it checked and telephone us as soon as they have the report."

"Right, sir!"

Roger replaced the receiver, told Venables, who looked boyishly excited, and restarted the engine. They were near Lutterworth and it was beginning to rain. There was much more traffic on the road, and Roger settled down again for a steady run on the middle lane. He felt a deeper satisfaction than he had for a long time.

Then he saw a van in the fast lane, overtaking.

It was just a van; very shiny black. He thought vaguely: pity it isn't grey. As it inched up he gave it a more direct glance. It drew level, and at that moment he saw the man at the van's open window, a pistol in his hand.

11

MOTORWAY

IT was a split-second of alarm, fear, swift and desperate action. Roger's reflexes worked without prompting, his foot went on the brake, the car wheels went nearly onto lock, the spurt of flame from the van was yards ahead, but the danger had only just begun. Somehow, Venables braced himself and stayed in his seat, but behind Roger was a car, now catching up with terrifying speed, and behind it a lorry, bearing down like a leviathan, and on either side a stream of cars of all shapes and sizes. He saw them swinging wide to avoid the car in front of him. The one immediately behind him was so close that a crash seemed inevitable.

The van was fifty or sixty yards ahead.

He put his foot down on the accelerator and shot forward, and the car behind fell away. The van seemed to fall back, also, and in a second or two they would be level again.

Venables was talking, radio-telephone at his ear.

"*Black Ford van, freshly sprayed, very bright, registration number XK 1497K . . . repeat, black Ford van, freshly sprayed, very bright, registration XK 1497K . . . approaching Lutterworth turn-off near Coventry over and out.*"

The van swung off the fast lane, on to the middle one. It was now so close it seemed impossible to miss. A little car with four people in it was on the slow lane. Roger swung in front of it, missing the black van by at most a foot, and quite suddenly they were alongside again.

The man still held the gun.

He fired, the bullet passing through Roger's car, striking the inside of the door post beyond Venables. Then the gunman dodged and Roger put his foot down harder and shot past. He cleared the black van. If he did what he wanted to now, he would pull in front of it, forcing the driver over, but if he did there would certainly be a pile-up and possibly several fatalities. They passed the turn-off at eighty miles an hour and at the same moment a voice crackled into the car.

"Patrol in front of you, sir. Scotland Yard's orders."

"*What shall I say?*" breathed Venables, then thrust the receiver out, mouthpiece towards Roger.

"West of the Yard," Roger said clearly. He was maintaining speed, a few feet in front of the van and saw the masked faces of the men in it. "Can you clear the road behind me? I want to force the van over." He spoke calmly, he felt calm, but there was cold sweat on his forehead and at his neck.

"Will do, sir. And another car will be with you about ten miles up."

"Thanks," Roger said fervently.

The patrol car dropped behind.

Venables put the receiver back on its hook but left the instrument switched on; there was squawking, talking, squeaking, the whirring of wheels. A few spots of rain struck the windscreen; all they wanted now was a wet road! The van was still twenty feet or so behind them. Suddenly a voice blared over a loudspeaker, clearly audible and understandable despite the other noises.

"All traffic pull into the verge and stop, please. This is a police order. All traffic pull into the verge and stop, please." The police car began weaving from lane to lane. "All traffic pull into the verge and stop, please." Cars started to pull over obediently. Two, on the fast lane, seemed to put on speed and flashed past Roger; the bloody fools, how did they know there wasn't an accident and pile-up ahead?

One of the passing cars, its windows open, was a Jaguar 3-litre, in black. Its nearside passenger had a cap pulled down over his eyes, his jacket collar turned up. The collar was blowing in the wind.

"My God!" breathed Venables.

The man's hand, clutching something that looked like an egg, appeared at the window. The cars kept even speed, now, only two feet between them. The man was going to lob the "egg" into or on to Roger's car.

Roger turned the wheel, and growled: "*Brace yourself!*" He kept both hands on the wheel as he pulled over. Before the "egg" left the man's hand the cars touched and wobbled, jolting their drivers and passengers. Roger felt the grating sound as side rasped against side, the jolt as handles met and were wrenched off.

"The "egg", poised for a final throw, was jerked from the man's hand. It fell back into his own car.

Roger almost stood on the accelerator. His car shot forward as the other swerved wildly. There was the second police car in sight, nearly a hundred yards behind. Roger drew clear. The Jaguar crashed into the dividing barrier, bumped off, struck again: and blew up.

One moment it was there, looking as if it would turn over as a whole, identifiable car. Next moment, it was a mass of flame and smoke, pieces of metal were flying in all directions, high into the air, into the barrier, over into the lanes of traffic travelling from the other direction. The police car disappeared, and for an awful moment Roger thought it had smashed into the Jaguar. But no: there it was emerging from smoke and steam.

The van was now two hundred yards ahead on a stretch of empty road. Venables was breathing very hard, gripping the handle of his door. Roger's teeth were gritting, his whole body was at almost unbearable tension, but he was gaining on the van, which seemed to be going at its limit.

The radio crackled, a man's voice sounded as if he were in the car.

"Leave this one to me, sir!" The police car flashed past Roger, who instinctively eased off the accelerator; but the tension was still there. He was aware of Venables' hissing breath; vaguely aware of the man's profile, of his lean body curved back against the seat.

The police siren was blaring out. The police car passed the van on the fast lane, then began to crowd it, risking a crash. The van veered over towards the slow lane, the police car kept pressing. They touched, swayed apart, touched again, but their speed was now much slower. Roger took the fast lane and passed. The police car was virtually nudging the van over, and as they slowed down another police car swung in from the opposite direction through a service gap in the barrier.

Venables was twisting round in his seat.

"Got 'em," he croaked.

Roger slowed down and pulled into the side, came to a standstill and then sat upright and unmoving. Sweat oozed out of every pore, enveloping him like a steam bath. He felt both boiling hot and icy cold.

It was hard to believe the chase had stopped, the danger was over for the moment, at least. He found that his jaws were locked; when he tried to move, his legs were, too.

Venables was staring at him.

"You all right, sir?"

Roger managed to nod.

"I'll see what damage we've done," Venables said. He got out, leaving the door wide open. Cool air swept over Roger. No cars passed. Venables appeared at the open window, then stood back in amazement. "Lost the handle, clean as a whistle, but apart from that just a few scratches," he reported. He was staring very intently at Roger, had obviously gone round to the other side for a closer look.

Roger's tension was oozing slowly out.

He raised a hand in acknowledgement, and looked in the driving mirror. Two policemen were on one side of the van, one on the other; the fourth was probably behind. One man was climbing down from the van; he appeared to be little more than a youth. A girl followed him.

"Get in," Roger ordered, and Venables nipped into the back. Roger reversed the intervening hundred yards, and stopped close to the little knot of vehicles and people. He got out, Venables grabbing at the door, and approached the police and their prisoners. The fourth man was at the back: he appeared as Roger drew up. Traffic was streaming south towards London, on the other side of the barrier, but this side of the motorway was like a desert of bitumen. One of the patrol policemen said:

"Mr. West?"

"Yes," Roger said. "Thanks for your help."

"Glad we were able to do a good job," the man said. "What shall we do with this pair, sir?"

The youth, bareheaded, his jacket collar rumpled, was startlingly dark-haired; and now it was obvious that this colour was dye. He had a fresh complexion and pale blue eyes, and his lips were almost baby-like; petulant. He couldn't be much more than twenty-one or two. Nor could this girl, who was probably younger. She had mousy-coloured hair, a rather bad complexion but quite beautiful grey eyes.

"Take them both under close guard to the station," Roger said. "I'll be back in a few hours, and will take them on to London — when you've sorted out the priorities. The charge concerns the shooting in Marley Street, London, last night, and the death of a policewoman as a result of an attack by this man and this woman."

As he was speaking, the girl wrenched herself free. Without a word and without any change of expression, she leapt at Roger. He was taken off his guard, flinging his arms up in front of his face as her fingers clawed at him. He felt sharp nails pull at his coat, felt the toe of her shoe kick at his shin. Then the policeman yanked her back. There was a flash and a click of handcuffs.

She glared, but didn't speak.

"And I'd like you to examine the van on the spot and then have it towed to London," Roger went on as if there had been no interruption. "What we'd most like to find are gold filings or gold dust, splinters or fragments of glass or powdered glass." He was being very precise, for there was some rivalry between the Yard and the provincial forces, and it was easy to tread on sensitive toes. While he was speaking, a radio squawked from one of the police cars. A man leaned inside to answer it. A moment later he bobbed out again, and said almost in awe:

"The chief constable, for you, Mr. West."

This would be the chief constable of the West Midlands region.

"Thanks." Roger took the instrument. "West here, sir."

"Superintendent," a man said in a deep and pleasant voice, "I know you are under pressure so I won't waste time. I've given my men instructions to co-operate with you in every way they can, and if you need to take or send the prisoners to Scotland Yard, go ahead."

"You're very good, sir."

"Anything you can leave to us, please do so," the other man said with a chuckle in his voice. "We will want to share in the reflected glory!" Then he went on in a flatter voice: "Will you come here or go straight back?"

"I'm on my way to Stone," Roger said. "I'd like to call on you when I'm on my way back."

"Do so if you can," said the chief constable. "Oh! I've a murder squad and some experts on the way to go over the wreckage of the car which blew up. Do you think they were the Bullion Boys themselves?"

"I don't know whether to hope they were or not," Roger replied. "Thank you again, sir."

When he turned round, the prisoners were in the back of one police car and a policeman was squeezed in between them. Both prisoners were looking straight ahead.

"All right for us to go, sir?" asked the driver.

"Yes," Roger answered. "One of you will stand by the van until your C.I.D. men arrive, won't you?"

"Be sure of that, sir!"

Roger went slowly towards his own car, looked at the handle, looked over the top towards Venables, and was silent for what must have seemed a long time. He felt an inner tremor which he knew was the onset of reaction and he had to be very careful indeed not to let it take over from him. He needed some kind of rest, some kind of relaxation and only one way was open to him.

"Will you drive?" he asked Venables.

"*Glad* to, sir!" Venables moved to his side of the car in a flash.

The door would open only from the inside, as the handle had gone, but it closed without difficulty. Roger sat back. Venables started off with the smoothness of the good driver. Roger took out cigarettes and lit one; he smoked very seldom these days.

"Wouldn't like some coffee, would you, sir?" asked Venables.

"I don't think we should stop again," answered Roger.

"Oh, no need to stop," Venables assured him. "My mother always sends me off with a flask of coffee and a snack. Still thinks I'm a kid! It's in my case, sir, if you can get it from under the seat."

Roger found himself chuckling. That was almost as good as a rest.

Soon he was drinking his coffee out of a waxed cup and nibbling some home-made biscuits. Venables drank half a cup of coffee while driving. A Jaguar $2\frac{1}{2}$-litre passed on the fast lane, and Venables looked in the driving mirror.

"The road must be open again, sir."

"Yes."

"Quite a mess to clear up," Venables ventured.

"Nasty, yes."

"I gathered the chief constable was co-operative, sir."

"Very."

There were a few more minutes of silence; more cars passed, they began to catch up with slower traffic. The coffee had done Roger a lot of good, he felt better than he had since the moment he had seen the gun.

"Sir," said Venables.

"Yes?"

"Do you think they are some of the Bullion Boys?"

Roger stubbed out his cigarette, glanced at the other man, and answered:

"No."

"You *don't*, sir!"

"No," repeated Roger.

"But —" began Venables, and then fell silent.

"They missed last night and they near-missed this morning," Roger said. "The Bullion Boys are too smart for that. And I'm pretty sure the two prisoners are too young and inexperienced. I would say the

Bullion Boys hired them, and that they made both attacks for money."

"I see what you mean, sir. These two don't behave like practised crooks."

"I can't imagine the girl letting off steam like that if she were," Roger said, and smiled. "But I'm only guessing. Don't put any of this in your report!"

"I won't, sir. Er — what about the pair in the Jaguar?"

"Anybody's guess," Roger said. "The Bullion Boys have a lot of money to throw about, and it's surprising what some people will do for a few thousand. We might find something useful from the reports on the blown-up car and the van." He took out his cigarettes again. "Care to smoke?"

"No, thanks, sir. I don't."

"And I don't know that I really need another, either." Roger put the cigarettes away. "I'm going to sit back for twenty minutes."

"Very wise, sir."

Roger stretched out his legs, leaned his head on the back of the seat, and closed his eyes. The time had come for thinking, not talking. He was still amused by Venables, who in some ways was so naïve, and so liable to be easily impressed; his driving was like everything he did: thoroughly efficient. Roger went right back to the beginning of the Bullion Robbery, and every facet of what he had done and what had happened passed through his mind. One thing was absolutely certain, the robbers were desperate men, desperate because they feared the police were too close.

Obviously Angela Margerison could know something dangerous to them; as obviously, now, either he or Venables did, or these attacks would not have been made. And it was on this fact that he concentrated: what did he or Venables know which had forced the Bullion Boys to take near-panic measures?

No new ideas came to him as they drove north.

Now and again, he opened his eyes, to see the rolling countryside of the Midlands, the trees nearly bare of leaves, the clouds heavy with threatening rain. Soon they turned off the motorway, and he sat up; but he was frowning again in concentration when a few miles along Venables announced: "There's the K & K van, sir. Now we won't be long."

12
K & K

THE van driver was by the side of his cabin, beneath the bright blue K & K painted an off-white. This was a Vauxhall van, not a Ford like the other, and when Venables pulled up the driver tossed away the stub of a cigarette, and said:

"You from the Yard?"

"That's right," said Venables.

"Just follow me, then." The driver clambered back to his wheel and led the way along a narrow road winding through clusters of modern houses, then turned off, towards meadows and trees. From a slight rise in the land, the factory gradually became visible. It was a vast building, no part of it more than two storeys high, set amid attractive grounds, with flower beds and shrubberies and huge sweeping lawns. Two gardeners were busy. The van stopped at a gatehouse from which two men came, checked their identity, and sent them along a wide road, past several car parks and a single-storey building. The van pulled up outside a larger, two-storeyed building. This, like all the rest and like the grounds, was immaculate. As the police car stopped a man came from some swing doors: brisk, pale-faced, rather tired-eyed. The van driver jumped down to open the door on Roger's side, and Venables got out quickly.

"Mr. West?" the newcomer asked.

"Yes." They shook hands. "And this is Detective Officer Venables." There was more hand-shaking.

"I'm Tolliver, P.R.O. for K & K," the newcomer volunteered, "and while we aren't expecting to cash in on publicity, I'm probably the man who can guide you around best."

Roger thought: Not Crabb?

"Mr. Crabb's on a long distance call — New York, in fact — or he would have been here to welcome you." Tolliver had a pronounced Mildand accent and his voice gave the same tired impression as his eyes. "He should be through by the time we're upstairs." He looked at the van driver. "Okay, Smart, thanks."

"Sir," said Smart, looking at the damaged side of Roger's car.

"Yes?"

"We could put a new handle on the superintendent's car in half an hour or so." His gaze turned to Roger eagerly, hopefully. "We've four Rovers and we keep a good stock of spares and parts."

"Would you like — " began Tolliver.

"I'd be very grateful," Roger said.

"Must have got very close to something," observed the driver.

"Another car, wasn't it, Venables?" Roger said.

Venables stared; and then suddenly burst into laughter. The laughter hadn't quite worn itself out when the van driver took the wheel of the Rover and the others moved towards the swing doors, Venables carrying Roger's case. The hall was very contemporary, with tropical plants and a small fountain. There was a flight of open, wooden stairs. A tall girl in salmon-pink, slim but well-curved, walked down with great precision, aware of the men and deliberately drawing their gaze. Venables took one glance and then stared at her face; she wasn't really pretty, but her figure was positively voluptuous. She did not look round as the others went up the stairs.

One of several polished brown doors opened, and another girl appeared, of more solid, less inviting mould.

"Mr. Crabb has just finished," she said. "Please come in."

They were hardly inside a small but pleasant office, with an unlittered contemporary desk and a stream-lined typewriter, when yet another door opened, and a man stepped through.

Instantly, Roger was aware of a rare quality in him. It was in his eyes; in the set of his jaw and lips; even in his movements, well-controlled though they were. He wasn't particularly tall or large but was immaculately dressed, the jacket emphasising the breadth and depth of his shoulders.

He put out his hand.

"Mr. West? I hope this will prove another of your triumphs . . . Mr. Venables, I'm glad to see you . . . Gladys, coffee and toast now, please . . . Do come in . . . Do sit down."

The office beyond was divided equally; one part truly office with desk and chairs, the other a sitting room with enticing-looking couches and chairs. An L-shaped table of the same colour as the doors stood on wrought iron legs. About the room were rubber plants, their thick, smooth, oval leaves easily recognisable. There were plants, too, of other kinds, some which Roger didn't recognise.

"If you are at all like me," said Crabb briskly, "you like to get down to cases immediately — ah! I was sure you did. I have my chief chemist and my chief glass technologist available the moment you are ready, and the research laboratory is at your disposal. We can use a supplementary one if your problem takes long. What *is* your problem?"

Roger took out the plastic envelope with the splinter of glass, and handed it to Crabb.

"May I take it?"

"Don't cut yourself," Roger warned.

Crabb flashed a glance from eyes half-hidden by heavy lids, at Venables' sticking-plastered finger.

He parted the plastic envelope with speedy care, and as he did so the door opened and the girl Gladys brought in a laden tray; a breakfast tray, with toast, butter, marmalade and honey as well as coffee in a dark green percolator.

"Thank you, Gladys. We will pour out." Gladys went off with a backward glance at the intriguing object in her employer's hand. "Would you care to pour, Mr. Venables — and do please help yourselves . . . Ah!"

He had the splinter on the palm of his left hand, and with a flip of movement took out a pocket magnifying-glass and looked through it, now close, now farther from the splinter. Venables poured out, keeping an eye on the other. Roger watched with fascinated interest, took some coffee which he did not really want, and some buttered toast for which he was grateful. As he ate, Crabb pursed his lips and did not once look up.

Suddenly, startlingly, he said: "I know two pieces of equipment this could have come from. And it was made here from a glass ceramic which we are using experimentally on some kinds of test tubes and — particularly — some large crucibles. The trade name of the crucibles is spelt with a K: Krucible." Although frowning he was obviously absolutely sure of himself.

"So Appleby knew what he was talking

about," Roger said, fighting hard to keep the elation out of his voice.

"He usually does," Crabb said drily.

Roger sensed a tension in him; something which had grown since they had entered the room. He asked a question which would give him time to assess Crabb more closely:

"Is your identification positive enough for evidence in a court of law, sir?"

Crabb pursed his lips and hesitated for a noticeable time before answering:

"No. But we can soon run tests which are positive enough for your immediate purpose. Analysis of the glass will be a slow process, especially with such a small segment to work on, but — " He broke off. "Well, we can get you what you want, Mr. West — you were lucky with your splinter!"

Venables rubbed his chin with a plastered finger, without speaking, as Roger asked:

"Can you tell whether it was from a test tube or a crucible?"

"I should think so."

"Would it be strong enough to hold molten gold?"

"Oh, yes," answered Crabb. "Gold melts at — let me see — a thousand degrees centigrade more or less, and this stuff will take at least twelve hundred." Excitement suddenly broke through his professional calm. "Is this about the Bullion Robbery?"

"Yes," Roger answered flatly.

"Gladys said something to me about that when I came in," said Crabb. "I was rousted out of bed about four o'clock and had to rush to one of our customers — they had an explosion. I wanted to see the place while there was a mess. Not our fault, thank God, the name K & K still stands accident free. Haven't seen the newspapers," he added, inconsequentially.

"That makes three of us," Roger said.

"Gold," remarked Crabb. He leaned forward and dialled a number, and almost immediately went on: "Jimmy, we'll be down to see you in less than twenty minutes. I've a splinter here which could come from a Glaseram Krucible or test tube. How long will it take to check? ... Good. I'll send it down." He rang off, pressed a bell, and went on: "He can tell in fifteen minutes, using an oxy-propane burner. Ah. Gladys." The door opened. "Take this down to Dr. Zigorski yourself, personally. No other hand but his and yours must touch it!" He had the splinter back in the little plastic envelope, and the girl took it and went out. "What you do think it was used for, Mr. West?"

"I wondered if gold could be melted down in one receptacle and then poured off into a smaller one or into a mould for small ingots, which would be much easier to handle than bullion bars."

Crabb looked at him very steadily.

"I don't much like guessing," he said, "but yes. Glaseram is strong enough. Do you know what a glass ceramic is?"

"No," answered Roger.

"Hm. Well, in the simplest terms, it is a ceramic which can be worked and moulded like glass, and it is used where visibility at very high temperatures is needed. Industry is using more and more alloys and synthetic rubbers and materials, and in processing the analysts need to see what's going on. So metal containers are no use. One of our associated companies produces a glass ceramic we call Glaseram, and we make the equipment here — so far, mostly test tubes and Krucibles."

"How big are these Krucibles?" asked Roger.

"Say a small, square frying pan."

"And gold *could* be melted in the Krucibles and when molten poured into the test tubes to cool," Roger said. "The chaps I'm after would want to be able to see what they were doing — that the gold was ready to pour."

"It would take a fantastic time to melt a gold bar," Crabb protested.

"If they turned the gold on a lathe, they would have only shavings and the core or stub to melt. That would be much easier, surely."

Crabb gave a brief, quite charming smile.

"It would indeed. Now, it is time — "

The telephone bell on his desk rang.

"Gladys!" he called, and got up, with a slight effort. "I sent her out, didn't I?" He rounded the partition to his desk and picked up the instrument. "Hallo . . . Yes, hold on . . . Mr. West, for you," he called.

Roger put his coffee cup aside and went to the desk. This was probably the Yard, but it could be from Western Midlands with news of the prisoners or the van. He picked up the receiver and said: "West speaking. Who is that?"

"It's Colonel Johnson," said the chief

constable of the region. "I've two preliminary reports in, Mr. West, and I thought you should know about them at once. There was no sign of gold or powdered glass in the van; and certainly no gold shavings or filings; it was exhaustively spring-cleaned and I'm afraid the result is final."

"That I can imagine," Roger said. "Pity, sir."

"So far only superficial examination into the wreckage of the Jaguar has been practical," Johnson went on. "But we have found three identical objects; solid gold, cylindrical in shape — not unlike cigars with the shaped ends cut off. All were undamaged by the explosion. As far as I can see from the report in front of me, there is nothing else of significance."

Roger said softly: "*Very* many thanks."

"Pleasure," replied the other. "I can tell you that a modern plastic bomb was used and caused the explosion. The prisoners have been sent to the Yard."

"All I *can* say is — thank you again, sir."

"Glad to help," said the chief constable, and rang off.

Roger turned slowly. Crabb seemed as intent as Venables, obviously his manner had affected them both. Roger raised his hands in a rueful kind of gesture, and went to his chair and picked up his coffee.

"Cigar-shaped gold pieces," he said. "Found in the wreckage."

"Good lord, sir!" Venables gasped.

"Wreckage?" echoed Crabb.

"We were chased by a car which blew up," Roger explained, "and among the wreckage there were three of these gold ingots, cylindrical, rather like cigars with the shaped ends cut off." He sipped his tepid coffee, and leaned back. "Would your glass ceramic test tubes mould gold into that kind of shape, Mr. Crabb?"

Crabb said: "Yes." And he repeated: "Yes, they have the heat resistance and the shape. We are only now experimenting in the manufacture, until some weeks ago we had bought all our supplies. And I can imagine — " He broke off. "Why don't we go down to the laboratory, they'll have some there." He dialled a number on the telephone on the table, and almost at once went on: "I'll be down with the Scotland Yard men in a few minutes. Have some of our Krucibles and some Glaseram test tubes on hand, will you?" He rang off and moved towards the door. "Ready, gentlemen?" As they followed him, he went on: "We'll drive round to the main works entrance, there will be less walking if we do."

Roger nodded. Venables looked at Crabb as he went along as if propelled by a rocket, and then turned to Roger and gave an expansive grin. Soon they were outside the front doors. A large Rover was drawn up with a chauffeur by the door.

"Main works entrance, George," ordered Crabb.

They drove in the direction from which they had come, very slowly. The sun was now higher, lighting up the grass and flower beds to great advantage. A lawn mower rasped. A few men walked briskly. As they turned towards the biggest of the buildings, they passed four K & K vans and one articulated lorry, marked *European Chemicals Limited*, being loaded with big cardboard cartons.

"Big delivery on its way to Italy and Yugoslavia, dropping one or two items off in Austria," Crabb stated. "Do you know that over half of our production goes to export? Hope you'll have time to look round afterwards — don't hesitate to ask questions if they occur to you." He was already out of the car and passing the workers who were loading a very large crate marked: *Trieste Chemica Experimenta.* "That's a type of container used for heart transplant apparatus," he went on. "Our own design, we think the best in the world. Sell them all over the world, too, except the United Kingdom!" That remark seemed more philosophical than disparaging. He led the way past many more packages and crates, marked for places as far apart as Tokyo and Buenos Aires, then along what seemed to be walls of foam rubber. Soon they were passing men sitting at benches and blowing glass. Strange shapes appeared on some of the flasks; at one bench there would be flasks with one neck; at the next two; at the next, three.

They came upon a door marked LABORATORY, and Crabb pushed the door open and ushered the others in. One tall, grey-haired man was standing with a pleasant-faced, fair-haired girl. Both wore spotless white smocks.

The girl said: "Well, there *are* six missing. Jimmy, I made the count myself."

The man, who looked not unlike Toscanini, turned to Crabb, arms held up in gesture of surrender. He had full lips, sad eyes with dark shadows under them.

"So you come," he said in a deep guttural voice. "So I have to tell you, six of the Krucibles are missing. Six. No record, no sale, no nothing. Who would take zem? Can you tell me that?"

He looked from Crabb to Roger and then to an article on the bench which looked very much like heat-resisting glass with a pinky browny shade. It was, as Crabb had said, similar to a small electric frying pan. At one corner was a lip, from which liquid could be poured. The handle appeared to be a kind of asbestos; possibly heat-resistant.

"No, but we'll find out," Crabb said grimly. "Are any Glaseram test tubes missing?"

"I do not know, it would be easy for a box to be taken without them being noticed," answered the chemist. "In stock-take this would be found out but not otherwise. Tell me, please — who would take these things?"

His voice faded, but for a few seconds no one spoke.

13

MISSING EQUIPMENT

ROGER felt the familiar thumping of his heart at the moment of a breakthrough. *Six* of the Glaseram Krucibles — and what else? He made no comment but watched the other man's lined face, his almost tragic expression. He had never seen him before but yet there seemed a great familiarity about him, as if he belonged not only to the world but to mankind, carrying its sorrows.

Crabb said: "No, I can't." He shot a baleful glance at Roger, and spoke to Tolliver, who had appeared as if from nowhere. "Tolly, go and get Bell, will you?" There was an almost menacing note in his voice as Tolliver went off; it wouldn't be true to say that he went like a dog with its tail between its legs but he certainly disappeared in a hurry.

There was tension in this place; no one could fail to be aware of it. The tension was created not only by the missing equipment but the mood of the man Crabb, the attitude of the laboratory chief and of Tolliver. On an instant, however, the atmosphere changed, and Crabb put a hand on the older man's arm, saying:

"Jimmy, you haven't met Chief Superintendent West, have you — and Detective Officer Venables. Gentlemen, Dr. Zigorski, who is in charge of all our research. You might call Dr. Zigorski the inspiration of K & K." He squeezed the other's shoulder and then let him go.

"You are very kind," Zigorski said. "I am grateful for your coming, Superintendent. Otherwise this loss would not have been found." There was gentleness in his voice and in his manner which matched the deep sadness in his eyes. "How, please, can I help you?"

Crabb asked bluntly: "Can our Glaseram Krucibles and test tubes be used to melt down gold and drain it off to make blocks the size of cigars?"

Zigorski drew in a hiss of breath.

"Gold!" he exclaimed, and looked with sudden excitement and perhaps fear at Roger. "That is what you think? They were used to melt gold?"

"Yes," Roger said.

"My God!" gasped Zigorski. "My God!" He began to move about the laboratory office, waving his hands in the air almost like a conductor waving his baton in time of stress. "Yes, yes it could so be used. Since the Glaseram is so very strong. *Yes.* It could be done." He came to West and stood close to him peering up, and now excitement was in his eyes, all other expressions were lost in this. "You understand, the melting point is such that it would be possible. We need glass or some material that can be seen through. Is transparent, of course. Because there is the question of the colour. The colour must be seen, so that in some form of distillation we get a greater perfection of the end product. Sometimes this is liquid, sometimes it is gaseous. So here in the laboratory we use the special kind of glass ceramic. Into the basic constituent we put something else. This makes the glass very strong. It can resist heat to a very high degree — as in such domestic materials as ovenproof glass only much higher." He gave a swift, unexpected smile which took years off his age and had great charm. "It does not begin to become plastic in form, or mouldable, until fifteen hundred degrees centigrade. Above the melting point of gold, yes — and also steel and platinum. The Krucibles would be a great market success, that I have no doubt."

All this time the three men had been watching him closely; and all the time the excitement glowed in his eyes. Suddenly, he stopped, and the glow faded, the sadness returned. He raised his hands, palms facing each other, in a helpless gesture.

"And now — six have been stolen."

Tight-lipped, Crabb said: "And probably some test tubes." His mood appeared to change, too; once again he was the man whom the others here came close to fearing. "Where were they stored?"

"But in the main laboratory," answered Zigorski. "Come. I show you."

He turned and walked swiftly away towards a partly open door on the side opposite to the one through which they had come. He flung it open to reveal a long narrow room, the whole of one wall made of glass, supported by a skeletal framework of steel or plastic. Beyond was the green of meadows and of distant trees. In front of the window was a very long bench — sixty to seventy feet, Roger estimated. At intervals of three feet there were stools, all occupied by men at work. The bench and a rack beyond it were full of glass containers and pipettes of all kinds, from simple test tubes to elaborate containers with half a dozen necks or outlets. Gas jets hissed gently at every bench. At one, a man held a Krucible full of a heavy-looking liquid and was pouring it into test tubes which were held in a rack in front of him. It was easy to imagine that this was how the molten gold was poured.

None of the men looked round, but there were others at the far side of the room near a glass container which must be nearly as big as a forty-gallon drum, who glanced up and away with the self-consciousness of being watched. Facing the door where Roger now stood was a desk littered with oddments of glass, metal, paper, pictures; and behind this in turn was a huge cupboard with three pairs of narrow doors. Two sets of doors were closed, one was open showing a very modern burglar-resistant lock; a man and the girl who had reported the loss of the Krucibles were at this open door.

Crabb moved forward, just behind Zigorski.

Roger put a restraining hand on Venables' arm, and stood watching. Crabb seemed almost to have forgotten their existence, he was so tense and preoccupied by the theft. Now, most of the men, standing or sitting, were looking at the General Manager and the Chief Chemist.

Venables whispered: "What's on, sir? They seem very worried."

"Yes," Roger said. "We'll soon see."

"Do they think their people are involved in the Bullion Boys' robbery?" Venables sounded genuinely puzzled.

"I doubt it," Roger said. "They're worried about the loss of a new kind of heat-resisting glass equipment."

"Good lord, yes! Industrial espionage. It — " Venables forced himself to silence, and Roger released his restraining hand and moved forward. On shelves in the open cupboard were some white boxes, and Crabb took one of these down. He weighed it in his hand, and then turned slowly, as if at last remembering the policemen. But he was looking past Roger to a man who had just come in, followed by Tolliver. This man had the almost ineradicable appearance of an ex-policeman, big, powerful, deliberate, with eyes which seemed always steady and clear, as if they absorbed everything about them without actually looking for it.

Roger recognised him on the instant: this was ex-Chief Superintendent Bell who had been at the Yard until a few years ago. He had retired early and joined one of the private security forces. Now he walked firmly past Roger, without speaking, and on towards Crabb and Zigorski.

He drew level with them.

"Good-morning, sir."

"Good-morning, Bell — did you know of the loss of the Krucibles?"

"Yes, sir — Mr. Tolliver just told me."

"Had you any prior knowledge?"

"No, sir."

"Had you any suspicion that this wall cupboard had been opened?"

"None, sir."

"Had you examined it?"

"Twice daily."

"Did you check this morning?"

"Yes — at half past seven."

"And every day, you say?"

"Yes."

Roger was now moving much closer. The little scene ahead was in a way very familiar, it was the kind of interrogation which took place often between a junior officer and a senior one at the Yard. Crabb was obviously deeply disturbed, Bell was obviously on the defensive. All but three or four of the chemists about the room had given up all pretence at working and were watching and listening.

"Well," Crabb said, "six Krucibles have gone."

"So I understand, sir." Bell was level-voiced and, now that Roger could see his face clearly, quite expressionless. He always had been able to keep a poker face; it had never been possible to be even reasonably sure of what was passing through his mind.

"And you cannot give us any indication of when the theft took place?"

"Not at the moment," Bell replied.

Crabb raised one clenched hand to his chest, pursed his lips with the underlip jutting forward. He looked both aggressive and formidable as he turned his head towards Roger. "Superintendent, you may know ex-Superintendent Bell." He allowed only a moment for an exchange of courtesies, and then went on: "I imagine you have realised that the loss of these Krucibles could be very serious indeed. We — and our associates — expected to have the secret of the manufacture of the glass ceramic — Glaseram — for an indefinite period. They are going into production next week and we would expect hundreds of thousands of orders for them. If another manufacturer had advance samples it would be possible for them to analyse and make a glass and an instrument very close to ours, and so obtain part of the market. You do understand, don't you?"

"Clearly," Roger said.

"And when do *you* think the robbery took place?"

Roger said quietly: "May we talk about this in private, sir?"

"I have no objection to it being known that a certain theft of very confidential matter has taken place from this room." Crabb was even more aggressive in manner; suffering, obviously, from some kind of shock.

"Much of my investigation *is* confidential," Roger retorted.

For a moment he thought that Crabb, so used to getting his own way, was going to try to insist on having it now; but suddenly his manner changed, he actually gave a brief smile.

"Yes, of course," he said. "We will go into your office, Jimmy." He led the way, oblivious alike of those men who turned suddenly back to their job and those who continued to watch. Soon, the investigating group was gathered in the office, both doors closed on them. "Now, Mr. West, if you can help us to find out when the Krucibles were stolen we will be most grateful."

"I can only guess," Roger said, and smiled at Bell, "You know how good I am at that, Tinker."

Bell's expression relaxed for the first time.

"The famous Handsome hunches," he remarked. "Yes."

"Since the time of the big Bullion Robbery," Roger stated.

Bell's expression changed with almost grotesque suddenness; his mouth dropped open and he seemed to have been dealt a physical blow. Roger had seen him react like this before, whenever he was taken completely off his balance.

"My God!" he exclaimed. "You can't be serious!"

"Never been more so," Roger assured him. "It seems probable that these Krucibles are being used to melt the gold down and pour it into small moulds. We don't know for certain when the small ingots were first made, but knowing the Bullion Boys I would think they would have had everything prepared from the beginning. So they may have taken these a week or two before the robbery. On the other hand, it's equally possible that they started with something else and came to these things later."

Bell said: "But that's over six months ago!"

"Yes."

Bell swung round to Zigorski.

"How long have they been in there?"

"It could be eight or nine months," Zigorski said with dignity. "They were the first of the experimental Krucibles you understand. There were twenty-four done altogether and they were all stacked on these shelves, twelve in front, twelve behind. I did not need ever to take any from the back."

"Well, some were taken." Crabb seemed set on regaining the initiative which had been seized by Bell for a few moments. "The vital need is to find out where they went. If you are right, Mr. West, they may have been used simply for processing gold, not for industrial espionage. I hope very much you are right."

Roger said: "I'd like to examine the shelf."

They went back to the laboratory. Tolliver pulled up a chair, Bell another, and stood side by side with Roger on a chair. From behind, Roger realised, they must look comical. Bell was breathing heavily as they peered behind the dozen containers at the front to the blank spaces at the back. There were some small outlines of dust but nothing else. The simple truth was that from the ground no one would have the slightest reason to suspect that anything was wrong; only when one came actually to remove a box from the front row did it become obvious that the back of the shelf was empty.

"So long?" Bell breathed, and there was a baffled expression in his eyes. "We haven't a chance to learn anything from that cupboard." He climbed down, then gave Roger a hand.

The others were at the desk, Crabb squatting on a corner, Venables, Tolliver and Zigorski standing, Zigorski apparently very ill-at-ease. Crabb had obviously got himself under control and there was no aggressiveness or anger in his manner.

"What are the chances of finding out who took them?" he asked.

Bell said: "If they were taken six months or more ago, not very good."

"Do you agree, Mr. West?"

"Yes," answered Roger. "I'd say that's a good general answer. Of course, if one of the assistants in the laboratory stole them, he is no doubt feeling in a bad way at this moment, and some quick questioning might make him talk."

"Handsome," Bell interrupted, "the lab staff is constantly changing. There must have been three or four resignations and replacements in the past six months. Possibly even more. Isn't that so, Jimmy?"

But Zigorski was staring out of the

window into distant places. He did not seem to hear. Bell opened his mouth to speak again but Crabb raised a hand to stop him. It was very quiet. The stillness continued for a long time, and Bell shifted restlessly from one foot to the other, until slowly Zigorski turned to face them all. The sense of sadness, of tragedy, was even stronger in his eyes.

"No," he said, obviously answering Bell's question. "No. There has been only one change. One and one only. Waldmann. My protégé — Waldmann." He braced himself and looked very directly into Crabb's eyes. "Mr. Crabb, it is my responsibility. This man came to me with the recommendation of a friend. A Polish friend. I did not like and I did not trust him but I employed him. It is my responsibility. It is like everything I touch — damned." He paused, and no one interrupted, in those few moments it seemed as if he was the only man who mattered: "What can I do to undo the harm which I have done?"

Crabb said gruffly: "We can't be sure that Waldmann took them."

"Oh, yes, we can be sure," replied

Zigorski. "He was in much need of money. He asked me for five hundred pounds, and I could not lend him as much as fifty. He left, two or three days later. He told me he had got the money in advance of the salary of a new position. When I asked him what position, he said that he was to work for a company which refined gold."

As he finished, Zigorski placed the palms of his hands together, and slowly, slowly, shook his head.

14

WANTED MAN

QUITE suddenly and with great precision Roger's thoughts clicked into place. Since arriving here he had been watching, waiting, groping; now he knew exactly what to do and how to do it. Still watching Zigorski, he put his thoughts into the right order, and while the others were still caught by the old man's attitude, he said:

"Tinker, we want that cupboard guarded until the local police come and check for prints ... And we need everyone who knew Waldmann questioned, a complete dossier made up ... Dr. Zigorski!"

Zigorski started, and shot a glance at him.

"Do you have a photograph of Waldmann?" West demanded.

"Yes, I have."

"Here, or at your home?"

"One will be on file in the Staff Office," Bell put in. "With some basic details, too."

"Good. Mr. Crabb, may we second Mr. Bell to the police when they get here?"

"Of course," Crabb agreed.

"If I can talk to the police as soon as they arrive I'd be grateful," Roger said, and nodded to Venables, who stretched out his long arm for the telephone. "Dr. Zigorski — will you make a full statement to the police when they question you?"

"Yes," Zigorski promised hoarsely.

"Thank you. Now may I see one of the Krucibles in operation?"

"That is easy," Zigorski said.

"Superintendent, do you need me any more?" asked Crabb. "I should report this situation to my parent company at once. The call to New York that I made this morning was about the Krucible. We received an order on the understanding that we had exclusive rights to the instrument and the special glass from which it is made, and it would thereafter be manufactured under licence in the United States."

"May I call on you if I do need help?" Roger asked.

"Of course," said Crabb, then looked bodefully at Bell and at Tolliver, long, protracted stares in each case. "Give Mr. West and all the policemen who arrive *every* assistance and absolute priority, please."

"I will," said Bell.

"Very good, sir," said Tolliver.

"Inspector Martin on the line, sir," Venables called, holding out the receiver.

"Ah, good." Roger moved across. "Inspector Martin . . ." He made arrangements for a squad of police to come from Stafford, where the nearest major headquarters was situated, rang off, and sat on a corner of Zigorski's littered desk. He would have to wait until the local men arrived but now he was on edge to get back to London. Zigorski was at a grey steel filing cabinet, getting out some papers, his shoulders bowed. "Dr. Zigorski," Roger said, picking up the sliver of glass. "Can you analyse this and confirm beyond all doubt that it is from one of your Glaseram Krucibles?"

"There is no simple process," Zigorski answered. "But there is a flame colouration test which will show if it is one of this group of glass ceramics. It has certain reactions also to high energy radiations." He went to the small bench in his room and lit a burner; as it was turned higher the hissing grew louder. "Be careful, please — this is oxy-propane gas, it can hurt the eyes." He picked the splinter up in a pair of pincers, then laid it across the flame on a small triangle of asbestos. As he worked he became absorbed and the cares dropped away from him. The others crowded round. "Please," Zigorski said. "Put on protector eye shades. This is a special oxy-gas flame, and very bright." There were several pairs on the bench and all three placed them in position.

The hissing increased.

The flame, as it struck the glass, spread out over the sides and acquired a blueish glow but showed no sign at all of melting. There was a small gauge attached to the burner, a thermometer for recording great heats, and excitement grew as the needle moved.

Gradually, a pale blue-green glow appeared inside the splinter itself; it was quite beautiful.

Zigorski took off his glasses for a moment, but quickly replaced them. He glanced round at Roger.

"The green glow," he remarked.

Through the eye shades this was more blue than green, but Roger did not remove his. He saw the whole splinter gradually changing colour, a beautiful delicate shade of azure blue to green. Zigorski looked at the gauge, and nodded, then turned off the gas. The blue colour faded almost immediately, and when the three observers took off their eye shades, the splinter looked just as it had been, with sharp, slightly curved edge.

"It is Glaseram," he declared. "The Glass Research Association in Sheffield can give more extensive tests and analysis, but I am sure this came from one of our test tubes." He picked up a test tube and pointed to a clear K & K mark, in light blue, close to the lip. "It came from just such a place," he declared. "No doubt at all."

Into the silence that followed, for Roger a deeply rewarding silence, someone tapped at the door.

"There's a Chief Inspector Martin for Mr. West, please."

The motorway stretched out in front of Roger as he headed south, with cars and lorries dotting all three lanes. The sky had cleared to a perfect blue, not unlike that of the Glaseram under naked flame. Back at the factory the Stafford police were going through all the routine, and by the time Roger reached the Yard, preliminary reports would be in. There was still an outside chance that Waldmann wasn't the right man but that was most unlikely. By now a full description of him, with his last known address, was at the Yard, and the nationwide search for him would begin.

Roger was driving on his favourite middle lane.

"Excuse me, sir," Venables said, after a spell of silence.

"Yes?"

"There's one thing that puzzles me."

"Only one?" Roger asked drily.

"About this particular aspect, yes, sir," answered Venables solemnly. "How would Waldmann know that the very thing he wanted was at K & K's? It could hardly have been a coincidence, could it?"

"I would take a lot of convincing that it *was* coincidence," Roger agreed. "However, it doesn't seem vital at the moment, unless you mean that there could have been a leakage at K & K in time to tell the Bullion Boys that suitable equipment was at the factory."

"That's what I do mean," said Venables, eagerly. "So there might be another lead from K & K to the bullion thieves."

Roger said heavily: "Yes." Then he glanced at Venables and went on: "If we can get Waldmann quickly we should be able to get all the information about K & K from him. If we start looking too obviously for another man at K & K we'll scare him away."

"So you *had* thought about it, sir?" Instead of sounding crestfallen, Venables seemed delighted.

"Yes," Roger answered drily, and went on. "The important thing is that you did, too, without a hint from me. How long have you been studying detection and deduction, Venables?"

"Oh, all my life!" Venables answered. "Anything that doesn't fit into a neat pattern always sticks out like a sore thumb to me. I've always been fascinated by puzzles of every kind. That's why — that's why the Force is so vital to me, sir. I hope — I hope to God I won't have to retire because of that — er — squeamishness."

"So do I," Roger said. "You could make a first-class detective."

Instead of making any immediate comment, Venables turned his head and stared straight ahead. The swish — swish — swish as they passed cars was like a refrain. They passed the spot where the Jaguar had blown up, and Roger began to ease off for the Lutterworth turn-off. At last, and very slowly, Venables replied:

"Forgive me for asking, sir, but you really mean I could become good?"

"Yes, I think you could," Roger answered.

"I — I appreciate that very much, sir."

"The Yard needs good men for the C.I.D.," said Roger, a little at a loss because of Venables' manner and his own talkativeness. Was he overpraising or simply encouraging the other?

"I know it does, sir. But not every senior officer would be so — so encouraging," Venables remarked. "As a matter of fact I'm used to being told not to be such a clever beggar. Mr. Know-All's been my name at Division for years." He gave an explosive laugh. "I've never learned how to keep my mouth shut," he admitted. "But I *can* learn that. The other — you'd be surprised how it scares me, sir. When you sent me over to get those spades yesterday my stomach heaved at the very thought of what we might find buried."

"No one really likes it, you know." Roger made the turn-off, and almost at once spotted a police car near the big roundabout; he slowed down still more. This wasn't the time, after all, to tell Venables what he had discussed with Appleby, for a policeman was already getting out of the patrol car. "Well, we've a welcoming party. Everyone's being very helpful."

"After last night do you think there's a policeman in the country who wouldn't give his right arm to help you find the Bullion Boys?" Venables said.

Roger grunted: "Probably not. While I'm with the Chief Constable, you check with the Yard, will you?"

"I will indeed," Venables said with obvious satisfaction.

Colonel Johnson, at the new Regional Police Headquarters near Coventry, was a tall, very handsome man with bushy moustaches. He sat at a new desk in a modern building, with a dozen or so little plastic bags on a side table near him. He had a hand grip like a vice.

"Very glad you could look in, Superintendent. How are things going?"

"Well, I think," Roger replied cautiously.

"They can't go too well," said Johnson. "Now! What about these?"

"These" were the cigar-shaped gold ingots which lay on his desk. They were side by side on a small black tray which threw their lustre up into relief. It was hard to believe that they were really gold. Roger glanced at Johnson, with his eyes raised, and Johnson said: "No prints on them. We've checked thoroughly." Roger picked one up. It was much heavier than he had expected but easy enough to lift and to hold. It was beautifully moulded, and as he balanced it on his palm he took out some of the small test tubes which Zigorski had made. He placed the ingot into the tube and it was a perfect fit; there was just room for it to go in and to fall out when the tube was turned upside down.

"You really have made progress!" exclaimed Johnson. "Does that mean you know where they melted the stuff down?"

"I think so," Roger said, and handed the mould to Johnson. "The tubes come from a glass products manufacturing company in Staffordshire."

Johnson nodded. He seemed as anxious as Roger to get going. He crossed to the side table.

"It's all marked — dust, paint scrapings, skin, hair, a fragment of a dental plate. You can go in and see our chaps at work on the rest, if you like."

"I'd rather send a man up later," said Roger.

"Then do that."

"Is there any indication of the nature of the explosive used?" Roger asked.

"Only that it is a plastic type. You have better experts on explosives than we have. If we could borrow one it might quicken things up."

"We'll send one," Roger promised. "You're extremely good, sir."

"We'd be glad to help, anyway," answered Johnson, "and now that a policewoman has been murdered — " He watched Roger putting the little plastic bags into his case as he went on: "I am a great believer in a Federal Police Force," he went on. "A central or Federal C.I.D., at least. We're much closer to it these days, but I hate to think of what we miss because there are so many separate forces." He watched Roger put the ingots into a separate compartment of the case. "Do you have any ideas on it yourself?"

Roger smiled.

"Everyone at Scotland Yard thinks a central force a good thing, you people out in the provinces are usually a lot less enthusiastic. But as a matter of fact, sir, I — " He hesitated and his smile grew sharper. "This is in confidence?"

"Of course."

"I was going to say that the main obstacle seems to be the Home Office," Roger went on. "Although they officially favour integration there seems to me a lack of enthusiasm there, too." He broke off, closing and then locking his case. "Which is hardly an active C.I.D. man's business! Well I know one thing: if we were a national force with headquarters in London I couldn't have had more co-operation than I've had today."

"Common purpose," murmured Johnson, and shook hands.

Venables was downstairs in the main hall. The car was parked outside. They went out together watched by uniformed policemen and two men who came hurrying forward, one of them with a camera. He should have expected it, West thought; this morning had been remarkably free from the newspapers. He answered a dozen questions and was photographed half a dozen times, then drove off.

A police patrol car followed.

"Well," Roger said, "anything from the Yard, Venables?"

"Nothing really new, sir," Venables answered. "But all the reports are in, all the lab reports too. No doubt that the gold filing was South African and the Johannesburg man still thinks they could even identify the mine the ore came from . . . Mrs. Margerison, no change . . . the young man and woman have been questioned for an hour but won't even give their names . . . No identification of the driver and passenger in the Jaguar yet, but there really hasn't been much time. If we can find Waldmann quickly, we'll get the best results, won't we?"

Roger said: "Yes, He — "

And then he whistled, and beat a tattoo on the steering wheel with his fingers. Venables was almost open-mouthed in his eagerness to know what was in his mind.

"What is — " He broke off. "Sorry, sir."

Roger kept drumming on the wheel. He was remembering the black hair and eyebrows of the driver who had attacked them on the way up. He wished he hadn't been in such a hurry to get away from K & K. He wondered whether Waldmann's photograph would be at the Yard by now. Then he waved his drumming hand towards Venables, saying:

"Call the Yard and ask them to make sure that staff photograph of Waldmann is there when we arrive. I can't wait to see that man's face."

15

WALDMANN

AS Roger's car turned into the driveway outside Scotland Yard, a crowd mostly of men, but with a woman here and there, surged forward. High on the roof of a parked B.B.C. van there was a television camera; another one stood on some scaffolding opposite the main entrance. Samuel Gaddison of the *Globe* who had been so full of critical questions the previous night, was close to the front of the crowd. Roger realised with a start of surprise that he hadn't looked at a newspaper all day. A small group of uniformed policemen and several C.I.D. men forced their way through and made a path for Roger, as Venables slid over to the driving wheel and, sounding scared, said: "I'll put the car away." Roger, a policeman on either side, had to go a step at a time towards the Yard, and a policeman said in disgust:

"Give me the bloody Ban the Bombers all the time."

Gaddison called out: "Were you hurt, Handsome?"

Roger forced a smile. "No."

"Must have come near it," remarked a C.I.D. man.

"How far away were you when the car blew up?" a woman called and he remembered seeing her last night, too.

"Near enough to feel the heat," Roger answered.

"My God!" a man breathed.

"How many shots were fired?" another demanded.

"I think there were three. If you want to see one of the bullet holes look in the door of the car."

"The car you've just arrived in?" Gaddison called out.

"That's the one."

All the time the cameras were clicking and flashlights spitting and the news cameras whirring. Why he hadn't expected it, Roger couldn't imagine. The M1 chase, the shooting, the burnt-out car, held just the excitement and news value that Fleet Street needed. Then he saw Coppell standing inside the open doorway of the Yard; the hall seemed fairly empty except for the usual staff and some C.I.D. and uniformed men. Roger, still protected on either side, was suddenly propelled into the hall, and came to a standstill only a few feet in front of Coppell.

"Quite the hero," Coppell observed, with a twisted grin.

"Anyone who has pushed through that mob is."

"Come off it," said Coppell. "Damned good job, Handsome."

"Oh, I didn't — "

"That won't wash," Coppell said. "I've got news for you. Coming up behind you was a Press photographer and a television cameraman — they were on your heels. What happened on the motorway will now be preserved in glorious Technicolor. No way of avoiding being a public hero, this time." There was grudging admiration in his voice, and in his expression as he turned towards the lifts, Roger alongside. "Where's that young copper you had with you?"

"He was so scared by the crowd he decided to put the car away."

"Lot of good that will do him," Coppell leered. "The garage has newspapermen hiding behind every car and a camera at every car window. There are even a few coppers down there." The lift stopped at the laboratory floor. "What's that about gold cigars?"

Roger said. "Give me a chance to open my case, sir, and I'll show you one. Has the photograph of the man Waldmann arrived yet, do you know?"

"Yes," answered Coppell. "It's your Waldmann. The black-haired killer."

"My God!" breathed Roger. "So we've got him."

"*You* got him." They were walking along the passage towards *Fingerprints*, which had its own mini-laboratory, and took up a large part of this floor. The department was in constant touch with the big laboratory at Holborn. Coppell stopped to face Roger, looking at him very straightly. "You've got a new image to live up to — don't forget it."

"A new what?" Roger asked, blankly.

"The *Globe* image," Coppell answered. "Don't tell me that you haven't seen it!"

"I haven't seen a paper today," Roger told him.

Coppell gave him a long, appraising stare, and then clamped his big hands on his shoulders, the first time Roger could ever recall him doing such a thing.

"Handsome," he said. "There isn't another man at the Yard who wouldn't have grabbed every newspaper on the bookstalls to see what they did to him after last night. The trouble with you is that you're too good to be true."

"I had a lot to do," Roger protested.

"I daresay. Well, you had a good press. The *Globe* pointed out that in view of the work you do and the fact that we're so understaffed it's a miracle that more wrong decisions aren't made. Instead of tearing your guts out for taking the tail off Margerison's wife, they have given you full marks for what you have pulled off. The Commissioner was so pleased he nearly came to the Handsome West Reception Party himself, but I had to stand in for him." Coppell took his hands away, but didn't move towards *Fingerprints*. "About this Waldmann."

"Yes?"

211

"I had a go myself, but couldn't get a word out of him."

Roger had a swift mental picture of that dark-haired youth and the sneering expression, and said:

"Can't say I'm surprised, sir. What about the girl?"

"The same."

Roger pulled a face.

"I'm not surprised about her either. I'll have a go later, if I may."

"You have as many goes as you like. Now let's see what the lab's got in store for us. Never known the Yard busier or the lab so eager to please us," went on Coppell in his more familiar half-jeering way.

Roger said: "Everyone feels the same, thank God."

There was a message for Coppell at *Fingerprints*: could he and Mr. West go to Holborn where they could see the whole picture.

"Mr. Smythe says he has some information about the piece of glass and some of the other stuff, analysed from the house and the van that was stopped this morning," the *Fingerprints* man added to Coppell.

"To impress the lab with the importance

of the situation I think I should come and give you some moral support," Coppell declared.

In fact the Commander's presence could put men on edge; make them tongue-tied. On the other hand if there was the slightest rumour going round that he and the Commander were at loggerheads, going in together could only be of benefit. Soon they were in Coppell's chauffeur-driven car, approaching the big skyscraper where the Forensic Science Laboratory was housed. Coppell chose to go straight up to the laboratory, not through the police station. The laboratory here had some similarities with that at K & K. There was the same long bench, flanked by a few cubicles. In one of these was a pile-up of every conceivable kind of article, suits, vacuum cleaners, shoes, hats, bottles, glasses, bags of dust, plaster casts. Each of these was labelled, each was to be analysed because each might yield a clue leading to the solution of one crime or another.

Chief Superintendent Smythe, tall, lean, thin-faced, was with them in a matter of seconds.

"Commander. Superintendent. Glad

you're here, and thank you for coming." He moved towards one of the cubicles, where a little man with pebble-lensed glasses stood at a bench with all the apparatus of a small laboratory, even to an electric oven. On one side were about twenty or thirty plastic bags filled with dirt and dust; on the other were smaller bags, more like the little envelope Roger had carried the splinter in.

"Mercer," Smythe said. "We want to know exactly what you've found, and we haven't a lot of time."

"Right!" The man was brisk with a resonant, echoing voice; a no-nonsense kind of voice. "On the left are the original samples. On the right, smaller samples after analysis. They are from the house and garden known as 17, Lyon Avenue, Chiswick, the green Morris Minor JLT 5123, the black van XK 1497K now in the garage downstairs." He picked up a sheet of paper. "This is the report on 17, Lyon Avenue; other reports are in the process of typing and will be here shortly." He paused for breath, looked up over his glasses, and went on: "Filings of South African gold found behind the wainscoting in room where a heavy machine was installed." He touched a tiny bag. "A minimal amount of gold dust not large enough for us to analyse here." He touched another bag. "In the same room as the gold filings were found, a minute quantity of a barbiturate powder was found, probably from a tablet dropped on the floor and chipped." He touched yet another bag, and looked up. "This is not strictly laboratory business but I understand that the supply of gas to the house has been some two hundred per cent higher than that of a domestic household of the same size, suggesting a non-domestic use of some significance."

Coppell interrupted: "Such as a laboratory or workshop?"

"It could be, sir."

"Fit in with what you know, Mr. West?" asked Coppell.

"If the gold was melted down in a flask or flasks supplied unwittingly by K & K the processing would need a constant supply of gas, but some extra heat — say heat from oxy-propane or oxy-acetylene would also be needed." Roger said, "We may need to come back to this and we may need it as supporting evidence in court. For now it's enough to know that there isn't any substantial doubt that the Lyon Avenue house was being used by the bullion thieves and that something scared them away."

Coppell grunted, then said to the chemist: "Go on."

"Right! Nothing else of the faintest significance was found in the house, which was freshly painted and polished after a thorough washing with strong pine disinfectant. There are traces of the disinfectant, dried out, in both lavatories. The paint and wax used is being analysed. Now for the garden — "

Roger felt his muscles go tense.

"There is conclusive evidence of work done by a very knowledgeable gardener," the little man went on, touching other, larger bags. "These are samples of humus taken from various beds, all plants — roses, apple trees, pear trees, hydrangea, rhododendron and others — having recently been fed with artificial fertilisers, all identifiable. Tags have been found on some of the trees showing date of treatment, and these tags, all green, are supplied with bags of the various fertilisers made by the firm of Lovelace of St. Albans, and having the trade name of *Gardluv*. There is some evidence that bags of the various fertilisers have been buried in a corner beneath a heap of burned garden rubbish and documents. These last are on their way here for analysis."

At last, he stopped, and Coppell said almost in an aside: "So you're on to your gardener, West."

"Looks like it," Roger said, and went on quickly: "What about the van?"

The chemist touched another bag.

"There was garden soil as well as house dust in some cracks in the floor, and also some traces of *Gardluv*. No gold dust or filings have been found, but traces of a fine canvas suggest that the inside of the van was lined."

As he finished speaking, a girl appeared, carrying a sheaf of papers, Smythe took these and handed them in turn to the man with the pebble-lenses, who put them on the bench and said:

"The other reports, sir. I would like you to check them before sending them down."

"Do just that," said Coppell. "Anything more for us, Mr. Smythe?"

"Not yet," Smythe said, stiffly.

"Let Mr. West know if anything turns up." Coppell moved away, then turned back to face the little chemist, who throughout had shown a kind of defiance, an "I'm-as-good-as-you-are" attitude. The expression was still on his face as he looked up at Coppell who was at least a head taller.

"You're Henry Mercer's son, aren't you?"

Startled, the man said: "Yes, sir."

"He was a good analyst, too. Is he still alive?"

"Oh, yes — seventy-seven and still going strong."

"Give him my regards," Coppell said. Roger caught a glimpse of Mercer's astonished expression, all suggestion of defiance and conflict gone. Smythe raised his eyebrows, echoing the astonishment. Coppell went out into the passage, holding the door for Roger. "Well," he said with a wry smile, "it looks as if what you want is an expert gardener who is also a machinist, a house-decorator and possibly a chemist." He paused. "Anyone in mind?" he asked as they got into the car.

"Women did the gardening, we know that," Roger said. "I want to see Waldmann, but I ought to get a bite of something to eat and take it easy for half an hour. There must be a way of getting at him so that he'll talk." They said little on the way to the Yard, and when they arrived Roger remarked musingly: "Gardener — chemist, that's what we want. Anything else you want me for at the moment, sir?"

"Have your meal," Coppell said. "I'd have it in your office if I were you, if you go down to the canteen you'll have everyone asking questions, or slapping you on the back."

"We can't have that," Roger said drily.

Coppell was being very human and, for him, gracious, a thing to be thankful for, but these facts slid over the surface of Roger's mind as he turned into his office. He pressed a bell for a messenger to get him something to eat, and sat back in one of the two armchairs usually reserved for visitors. There was a ceaseless pounding of ideas and facts in his mind, as if a pile-driver were at work. He kept seeing faces, too; those of Rose Nicholson, Angela Margerison, Zigorski, Crabb, Margerison, the black-haired Waldmann, the defiant girl, Henry Mercer's son. Of them all the most vivid pictures were of the dead policewoman, Zigorski and Waldmann. All the things Mercer had said remained vividly with him, also. It wasn't possible to be sure, but if he let all of these facts and impressions run through his mind he might well come up with an angle no one had yet seen.

There was a tap at the door, and after he called "Come in" it opened slowly, cups and plates rattling, as a tray appeared, clutched in a pair of very big hands. Venables prevented the door from slamming with his foot, and then placed the laden tray on an upright chair close to Roger.

"I happened to be outside, sir, and took this from the messenger."

"Where else have you happened to do or go?" asked Roger.

"Well, I did call the laboratory, sir, and Mr. Smythe sent the transcripts of the analysis reports over." Venables drew these from the inside pocket of his jacket. "I just managed to glance through them," he went on. "Very comprehensive, sir, aren't they. I — er I — " He broke off, looking quite embarrassed.

Roger picked up a thick beef sandwich.

He bit into it hungrily; it was after two thirty, no wonder he felt famished.

"Pour me out some coffee," he said, "and tell me what's on your mind."

Venables poured out black coffee and hot milk from different pots, and when he put the cups down, he said:

"Very lovely bed of roses outside the laboratory window at K & K's sir, wasn't it?"

Roger stared at him, and then exclaimed: "My God! They had *Gardluv* tags on them too." The camera part of his mind had registered that, but until this moment the computer part had not. "And Dr. Zigorski — "

"Is reputed to be fond of gardening, sir," Venables remarked. "It's at least possible that Dr. Zigorski knows much more than he's told us, isn't it?"

Roger looked searchingly into Venables' face, then said slowly. "You're right. We'd better have him down here — we can say it's to help identify Waldmann. Arrange it, will you? Talk to Mr. Crabb first."

16

CONFRONTATION

WALDMANN and the girl charged with him were in different cells at the Yard.

Zigorski was on his way down to London, in a police car.

Roger, still at his desk, had read the newspapers at last; the write-ups could hardly have been better, but there remained the knowledge that Rose Nicholson was dead because he had made a certain decision months ago.

He got up, suddenly, and picked up the telephone to the chief inspector in the next room.

"I'm going to the Map Room," he said, put the receiver down and went out of the office. Two or three people in the passages and at the lift nodded or chatted, but no one mentioned the Bullion Boys. He went down to the basement and stepped out into what seemed like a maze of maps. All of them were of different sections of London, all had varicoloured pins stuck into them, and each carried a legend to explain the colours. He knew the Map Room well, but only the staff here was really familiar with the maps. There were some showing the density of various crimes: drug-taking, car-stealing, shop-lifting, pocket-picking, bank raids, hi-jacking. Once one knew the key, it was possible to get a clear picture of London's crime from these maps alone. And concentrations of crime led to concentrations of police.

He looked into a small office where a man sat at a huge desk covered with smaller sections of maps.

"Spare me a minute, Jack?" asked Roger.

The other looked up.

"Hallo, Handsome! Didn't hear you!" He stood up. "What can I do to help catch the Bullion Boys?"

"I'd like a map section which has Chiswick about the centre," Roger said, "and I'd like to check the approaches to Lyon Avenue and to Chandler Street, where Mrs. Margerison lived — and I'd like to check places within easy reach of

Lyon Avenue where a piece of heavy machinery could be stored."

The other man was already opening one of the map drawers; and he placed a section on top of the sloping desk. The two men pored over it for some time.

"A suspect green Morris Minor and a suspect grey van have definitely been seen around Chiswick," Roger murmured. "They might still be in the area."

"Oh, yes: and that heavy machinery, too. Unless the piece was dismantled it would have to stand on a ground floor. Hundreds of houses and shops where it could have been taken. Didn't I see a request somewhere for places recently let or sold?"

"Yes," Roger answered.

"Well, why not get a list and then mark them off here," the Map Room Inspector suggested.

"Let me use your telephone," urged Roger.

Soon a list of the possible places into which the Bullion Boys might have moved was being marked with blue-headed pins on the section map. It made a pattern around Lyon Avenue, and Roger, who knew this part of London better than any other, watched the build-up. There were a dozen possible places in Hammersmith, several clustered around one spot to the right of Chiswick High Street. The most suitable appeared to be some railway arches used for small manufacturers — boat builders, motor repair shops, woodworkers, small tool manufacturers, radio and television repairers, trades in all variety.

"And all within half an hour's drive of Lyon Avenue," the Map Room Inspector stated.

"What's more no one would be surprised if anyone was working late there," Roger put in. "And the approach to the Arches is nearly cut off from main roads." He pursed his lips. "It's guesswork," he went on, "but — May I use your phone again?"

"Help yourself."

Roger called the West Division, and was quickly put through to the superintendent in charge. One thing was rewarding about this case; everyone without exception was eager to help and to give that help priority.

"Hallo, Handsome," the superintendent said. "Thought I'd hear from you sooner or later. I had a chit from you asking for any of our chaps who saw people moving about eight days ago."

"Yes," Roger said, sharply.

"Well, there was a move from 17, Lyon Avenue just a week ago," the man reported. "Your chap Green has established that. And we've a report from a patrol car about a move into one of the Arches at Hammersmith the same night."

"Have you had the place at the Arches checked?" Roger asked.

"No, just watched from a distance," said the superintendent. "Green's watching now."

"I'll go and see him," Roger decided. "Thank you very much."

He put the receiver down and had a momentary flash of exasperation because he hadn't been told this, but had had to dig it out. Then he laughed to himself; there had been so little time, the miracle was that so much was fitting into place. There was time to go out to the Arches and see Green and be back before Zigorski arrived; and he wanted another talk with Zigorski before he questioned Waldmann.

The Map Room Inspector was grinning at him.

"You'll burst a blood vessel one of these days," he said. "Have I helped?"

"You have a lot," Roger assured him. "You can help more, too. Draw up a plan so that we can watch everyone approaching those Arches. We want to make sure that no one can make a sortie and break out into Greater London."

"Give me half an hour," the Map Room Inspector asked modestly.

"Send it up to *Information* when it's ready, will you?" Roger asked. He hurried out, watched almost furtively by men at the big maps, and went up to his own office. Venables was sitting at a corner of the desk, reading typewritten reports.

"Any news of Zigorski?" asked Roger.

"Yes, sir. He'll be here in about an hour."

"We're going out to Hammersmith," Roger said. "Bring anything you want to talk about with you." He rummaged through his own files and then selected a form and filled it out. "We'll drop this into the Commander's office on the way," he went on, and handed the form to Venables. "Seen one before?"

Venables glanced down.

"A permit for a *gun*, sir?"

"Yes. We need it signed by a magistrate or J.P., and Mr. Coppell will fix it. You drop it into his office, I'll meet you in the garage."

"Very good," said Venables. "You really think — "

"If we catch up with the Bullion Boys we'll certainly need a gun," Roger told him.

Five minutes later he drove out of the garage, past a dozen or so newspapermen still waiting for news, then turned towards Victoria. Traffic was already thickening for the early rush hour, but he weaved between the traffic and in twenty minutes reached Turnham Green. He saw Green, with another man, standing by a car, and at the same moment Green saw him and came hurrying. There was a tense expression on his face.

"Get in," Roger said, and as the burly sergeant did so, he went on: "So you found out when they moved."

"More than that, sir," Green said, with suppressed excitement. "They're at Number 27, The Arches!"

Roger's heart was beating like a triphammer.

"No doubts?"

"Can't imagine any, sir. We had some luck. There was a nail in one of the tyres of the black van, sir — tele-picture was sent to us from the West Midlands."

Bless Colonel Johnson!

"Yes."

"We've found impressions of that very tyre and the nail outside Number 17, Lyon Avenue *and* on three places approaching the Arches and several on the path leading from Number 27. A grey van was parked there and so was a green Morris Minor — we've checked with a firm of engineers on one side and a fibre-glass boxmaker on the other. And — " Words were spilling out of Green. "And no one visits there by day, although one of the boxmakers on overtime the other night saw a couple go out the night before last."

"Couple?"

"A middle-aged couple, I'm told, who went to an Indian restaurant in the High Street."

"And the doors of Number 27 are closed now?"

"Yes, sir — the 'To Let' notice is still pinned to them, as if they want to create the impression that it's still empty."

After a long pause, Roger said: "So it looks as if we might have them."

"It certainly does!"

"Green," Roger said, "the Map Room Inspector is preparing a plan to blockade the Arches. You get it from him if it hasn't yet reached *Information* and then talk to Division and the Flying Squad. We've got rush hour on our hands and we don't want to start anything yet, but we want every possible exit from those Arches guarded, and everyone from them stopped and questioned."

"Will do, sir!" Green couldn't keep his voice level.

"But don't do anything to warn them that we're watching."

"Don't worry, sir, I won't. They'd kill any of us as lief as look at us — I won't take any chances."

"Right!" Roger said, and was reminded of Mercer at the Yard laboratory. And he was reminded of Green's limitations, too. Number 27 was next door to a firm of engineers, and at least one of the men at 17, Lyon Avenue had to know something about engineering. But if Number 27 was being watched the other Arches were, too.

Green got out, Roger drove slowly round Turnham Green, so that he did not have to cross the flow of traffic in order to get back. Traffic had grown very thick, and pedestrians were in their thousands. Before the night was out tens of thousands of people would pass within a few hundred yards of where the Bullion Boys were holed out. He knew there was still a possibility that they were barking up the wrong tree, but he was almost as sure as Green.

"How well do you know it here?" he asked Venables.

"Fairly well, sir — I spent the first year in the Force in this Division," Venables answered. "Those Arches are pretty old. Still cobbled, too. There's one thing sir."

"What's that?"

"There *is* only one way in and one way out, except over the top. Some of the Arches have iron ladders up to the railway line, which makes a pretty good escape. But Division will see to that, I'm sure." He paused, then shot Roger an almost pleading look. "You'll let me in at the kill, sir, won't you?"

"It may be a kill in more ways than one," Roger replied grimly.

"Oh, I know, sir. They might try to shoot or even blow their way out. But that's all in a day's work."

"Yes," agreed Roger. "Yes. And of course I'll want you there when we raid the place." He pursed his lips, and then said. "If we're really good we'll find a way of getting them out without a lot of trouble."

Venables didn't answer, which was a reasonable indication that he did not agree.

"Now!" Roger said briefly. "We want Division and the Flying Squad briefed, and we want anyone from the two arches on either side of Number 27 closely watched. Some of those arches have access to the ones next door, don't they?"

"Yes, *sir*," said Venables, with obvious relief. "I was worried about that engineering shop, but I needn't have been. Shall I call Division?" He stretched out for the radio telephone.

Half an hour later, Roger turned into his office as two telephones began to ring. He picked up the one from the Yard Exchange, said: "Hold on, please," and picked up the internal one. "This is West," he said.

"How did you get on?" Coppell wanted to know.

"We hope we've got them boxed in, sir — some of them, anyhow."

"Thank God for that. You can have your gun but don't use it unless you're forced to."

Roger said formally: "No, sir. I have wondered whether the Division and the Squad men watching the Arches should be armed. I've talked to the leaders of both, and told them not to hold or question anyone who leaves the Arches but to follow them. This could be a very big job."

"Use every man you need," urged Coppell. "Bring some men back for overtime if you need to. As for more guns — "

"The Bullion Boys may have some more of those explosive eggs," Roger reminded him. "The whole thing will need handling with extreme care."

"Don't I know it!" Coppell exclaimed.

"I'd like to discuss the situation in detail with you before we raid," Roger went on.

"When?"

"I would expect within an hour. I want

to see Zigorski and Waldmann first. They might say something that will help to minimise the risk."

Coppell said clearly: "Oh, hell." There was a pause, and when at last he went on there was a tone of resentment in his voice. "I'm beginning to understand why the wives of detectives go off the deep end so often. When will the raid be?"

"Some time this evening, I hope."

There was another pause, before Coppell said: "Of course we'll need some time together. And I'd better be there. Or at least at hand. All right. I'll send that gun permit along." He rang off, obviously in an ill temper, and Roger drew his hand across his forehead. Coppell with domestic problems was really something new. He picked up the other telephone and said:

"Sorry to keep you."

"It's the sergeant in charge of the waiting room area, sir," a man responded. "Dr. Zigorski has just arrived."

"Thanks," Roger said. The timing could hardly have been better. "I'll be along in a few minutes. Hold on." He pondered, lips pursed, chin thrust out, and then he went on: "Who is in charge of cells?"

"Sergeant Tandy, sir."

"Will you tell Sergeant Tandy that I shall be sending for the man accused of the M1 crimes any time now, and will want him in the waiting room with me and Dr. Zigorski."

"Very good, sir."

"And when I've done with the man I'll want to see the woman prisoner at the same place, but they mustn't meet."

"I'll see to it, sir."

"And Sergeant," Roger said grimly, "be very careful. I don't mind how many men you use but be careful. And keep the handcuffs on the male prisoner."

"I will, sir."

As Roger rang off, he looked across at the armchairs a little wistfully. The simple truth was that one needed time to think, time for the subconscious to do its work, and he simply wasn't getting enough. Only in recent years had he been aware of this, for most of his life he had been able to take whatever had to be done in his stride. Not now. And there was little doubt, he created many of his own pressures. He need *not* have rushed up to K & K. He need *not* have rushed out to Hammersmith. And it was almost certain that had he taken things a little more calmly, even spread the Midlands trip out all day and simply given instructions to have the Arches watched, the eventual result would have been the same. He simply pushed himself to the limit, and when one was stretched so tightly there was a risk of misjudgement and so making wrong decisions.

"Don't harp on that!" he admonished himself. "I'm going to see Zigorski!"

Going down in the lift he was actually whistling aloud. He walked briskly along to the waiting room. Nodding to the policeman on duty he glanced through the one-way window, just as he had done when he had gone to see Angela Margerison.

Now, he saw Zigorski, and had no doubt at all that the sadness and pain in the man's expression had merged together into absolute despair.

17
YOUTH V. AGE

ROGER went into the cool, barely-furnished room, where he had seen Angela Margerison and Policewoman Nicholson; that now seemed not a few hours but ages ago. In place of the policewoman there was a policeman, in his forties, comparatively old at New Scotland Yard. There was a hardness about him; about the set of his lips, and jaw, the expression in his eyes, the way his brows jutted and his forehead rose like a cliff beneath iron-grey hair. He was standing, arms behind him, as if in constant reminder that his companion was a captive.

Zigorski, seeing Roger, sprang up; the policeman's arms moved, he was set for action; at least he was quick to perceive that none was needed, that Zigorski offered no threat.

"Superintendent!" Zigorski cried, and there was an ache of reproach in his tone. "Why did you bring me here?"

"I'm sorry I had to," Roger said. "I have to know more about your friend Waldmann, and I couldn't come to see you."

"But I have told you all I can about him. I am terribly sorry that I gave him the position, that he appears to have abused it, but — "

Roger took the photograph from his case and held it out.

"*Is* that Waldmann?" he demanded.

"But of course! I told you so."

Roger placed the photograph of the girl on top of that of Waldmann. He had a sense of urgency, and of the real significance of what Zigorski knew, but he had no idea whether Zigorski was aware of that significance.

"Do you know this woman?" he asked quietly.

Zigorski backed away, groping for the arms of his chair. He actually began to sit down as Roger held the picture even closer to him. He averted his eyes, narrowing them until the wrinkled lids all but covered them.

"Who is she?" Roger asked.

"Please," Zigorski whispered. "Do not make me talk. Please, leave me in peace."

He covered his face with his frail delicate hands.

"Dr. Zigorski," Roger persisted gently. "When did you last know peace of mind?"

Zigorski's whole body stiffened. Roger still held the photograph of the girl who had rounded on him with such venom, but he did not speak. He was oblivious of the policeman, whose expression had changed and who now seemed deeply concerned in the conflict between the old man and Roger. The room was very quiet. A faint rustling of cloth as Zigorski lowered his hands from his face was quite noticeable.

"It was a long, long time ago," he said huskily.

"What broke your peace?" asked Roger, and he raised the photograph. "Did she break it?"

Zigorski stretched out his hands as if for succour, looked down at the photograph and then back at Roger. He had such beautifully shaped lips; and without the shadows his eyes would have been beautiful, too: like the girl's.

"You know, don't you?" he said.

"I think I know," replied Roger. "Is she your daughter?"

The policeman actually drew in a hissing breath.

"Yes," answered Zigorski, as if his heart would break. "Yes. She is my daughter and my only child. It was to help her that I gave Waldmann work; and it was to try to help her that I did not talk of the missing flasks. I did not know for certain what was happening. I did not know that Waldmann was involved in the gold robbery, until Crabb asked me if the Krucibles could be used for melting gold, and then — then I knew." He drew his trembling hand across his forehead, pressing hard with the tips of the perfectly shaped fingers. "At first I did not wish to face the truth. I told myself that he was going to sell the secret of the glass to competitors in the industry. I felt that if I betrayed him I would betray my daughter. Where did my loyalty lie?"

Roger placed the photograph on the table, and answered:

"Only you can judge yourself Dr. Zigorski. But much more is involved now. Waldmann and your daughter, together, have already killed one human being and have tried to kill others. And they have associates who will kill just as readily. You don't have any choice left, you have to tell the whole truth. You can't live with the lives of innocent people on your conscience."

"No," Zigorski agreed in his hopeless voice. "I cannot, knowing what you have told me. I can no longer lie to myself, so how can I lie to you? My daughter's name is Flora. She has been involved with Waldmann for many years. She is not — not as I would wish her to be. She has always been different. Sometimes it has seemed to me that in place of her mother's goodness, she was born with evil in her — "

She and Waldmann had been to see him several times, he went on to say, in his home near Stone. They had taken back fertilisers and plants from the factory, for Flora had one quality inherited from him: she had green fingers and was passionately fond of gardening. They had wanted to stay at his house but he had not permitted it.

"I knew, of course, that they were hiding from the police, Superintendent."

They had talked very little, simply come for a rest, and to borrow money; they came nearly always after dark and stayed for a day or even two, always leaving after dark...

"But I do not know where they are now, Superintendent, I beg you to believe that I do not know."

"Do you know any of their friends, or where they lived in London?" Roger asked.

"Their friends, No. But I do know that Waldmann worked for a while for a small firm of engineers, specialists in making machinery and tools which could not be mass produced," Zigorski replied. "And I know that this company had its workshop at a place called The Arches, in Hammersmith. Once or twice when he was working for K & K, letters were readdressed to him from the Arches, by his employers — *The Arches Tool & Machine Company*, Superintendent. I am sure they can tell you more about him than I can."

"I imagine you're right," Roger said, and moved away a little. He himself felt relaxed and tired, as if a great trial was over; an ordeal, too. "Will you make and sign a statement confirming all you have told me and adding anything more you might remember? The known addresses, for instance, the Christian and or surnames or anyone they knew?"

"I will, gladly," Zigorski promised.

"I'll send Detective Officer Venables to take the statement down," Roger promised. He looked into those sad but beautiful eyes and he thought that Zigorski seemed to have eased his burden by talking about it. The one question which must still haunt him was obvious: where was his daughter now, and what was she doing? "Dr. Zigorski," Roger went on, "I think you may be glad to know that your daughter is under arrest."

There was a long, long pause.

The policeman standing by smothered a cough, and relaxed, putting his arms behind his back again.

Zigorski nodded, very slowly, and closed his eyes; the tiny criss-cross of veins on the lids showed vividly, red and blue and mauve and brown.

"So she can do no more harm," he murmured.

"She might even do some good," Roger told him. "If she would talk freely, turning Queen's Evidence, she might receive a very light sentence and be able to start afresh."

"You are kind to consider it," Zigorski said, "but I do not think she would agree. I do not think she would ever harm her lover, Superintendent, because she loves him so deeply." Alarm shone suddenly in his eyes, and he went on: "Please! Do not ask me to try to persuade her!"

"No, I won't do that," Roger promised. "Just let me know if you would like to try. We may need you in London for a day or two, but won't keep you longer than we must. Would you like to call K & K, or shall I?"

"If — if you will tell them all I have told you it would be a great relief," Zigorski replied.

Roger nodded, turned to the door and looked across at the policeman. "Detective Officer Venables will be here in a few minutes," he said. "If you need to go off duty, arrange it with him."

"Thank you, sir, but I can see this through all right."

Roger nodded and went out.

Two policemen in uniform were outside, with Venables; Roger should not have been surprised that Venables was already at hand. All of them straightened up, and Venables looked eager.

"Dr. Zigorski will make a statement. take it down, will you?" Roger said. "And take it straight to my office and wait for me there."

"Very good, sir!" Venables could not get to the door soon enough.

Roger looked into the next and empty waiting room, and called the sergeant in charge of the cells. "I'm on my way," he said. "Is there any change of attitude in either of the prisoners?"

"None at all, sir."

Roger rang off, then beckoned a policeman as he went along the passage.

"Have some coffee and sandwiches taken in to Dr. Zigorski," he ordered, "and remember he is a witness, not a suspect." He went striding towards the lift, and was soon walking along the passage that led to the cells. Hovering at the back of his mind was the possibility that he could use Zigorski's story to make the prisoners talk, but there was at least a risk that it would make them even more stubborn.

The sergeant in charge of cells was a big, paunchy, gentle-looking man. He was waiting for Roger, with a constable just behind him.

"Good-afternoon, Mr. West. Haven't had the pleasure of seeing you down here for a long time. Great pleasure, sir. What I forgot to ask was, do you want to see those two one at a time, or as a pair?"

"I'll see them separately, the man first," Roger decided. "We'll go into the interviewing room, and I'll want at least two men in with me and a guard outside. They could both be deadly."

"We'll be careful, sir," the other promised.

The interviewing room was like the waiting room upstairs but had more furniture, a larger table, several hard-back chairs and a large desk with two telephones. Roger waited impatiently. One telephone tempted him to call K & K but there wasn't much time. At the back of his mind was the one preoccupation: how to raid Number 27, The Arches and how to make sure that there was no disaster. He stood facing the door when it opened and Waldmann came in with two uniformed policemen.

He was handcuffed to one of the policemen, and Roger said:

"Take the handcuffs off, will you."

"He's liable to be violent, sir," the man cautioned.

"We'll take the chance," Roger said, and

watched as the key was inserted and the handcuffs removed. Everyone in the room went tense as Waldmann flexed his arms and actually moved up and down on the balls of his feet, as if about to spring. The sneer on his face seemed engraved with a chisel on stone.

Roger took one of the "cigars" from his pocket and laid it on the table. Catching the light as it turned, it rolled along the table towards the prisoner.

Waldmann's stare instantly became one of great consternation.

First sight of the ingot of gold had punctured the bravado, and he had watched the rolling ingot with bulging eyes. As if hypnotised he continued to stare at it when all movement had ceased. Five seconds of utter silence followed; then Roger posed his question.

"How many of those are there at the Arches?"

Waldmann's gaze darted from the ingot to Roger. Roger was ready, but had Waldmann chosen that moment to try to attack them, he might have caught the others unprepared. Instead his mouth dropped open, his whole body sagged, as if that was the moment when he first realised how utterly he was defeated.

"Frederik Karl Waldmann," Roger said in a sharp voice, "I am a police officer and it is my duty to charge you with the murder of Police Officer Rose Nicholson by shooting her during the hours of daylight yesterday the 17th November, in Marley Street, London, W.1." He paused long enough to see the shock reaction in Waldmann, who until then had believed that his identity was unknown. "It is my further duty to inform you that anything you may say will be taken down in writing and may be used in evidence at your trial." He paused again and then asked sharply: "Have you anything to say?"

Waldmann opened his lips as if with great effort; and then with the same effort, closed them again. Shock still showed in his eyes, it would surely take little more to make him talk.

"Flora Zigorski will also be charged," Roger stated.

Waldmann seemed to bite the inside of his lips, to stop himself from talking. Where another man would surely have blurted out that she hadn't used the gun, that she had played no part in the killing, he still kept silent.

"What are the names of the two men who were killed when the Jaguar blew up on the motorway?" Roger demanded.

Already, he was beginning to feel that the moment had passed when this man's resistance could be broken down. And there was a change in the attitude of the policemen, too; eagerness, hopefulness, had faded. One, with a notebook and pencil in his hands, had already taken down every word Roger had said, and now he waited, watching Waldmann.

Out at Hammersmith, Roger knew, people were watching the Arches.

Somewhere upstairs Coppell was waiting, undoubtedly with growing impatience and probably with exasperation. And here a man who could tell him so much stood as if he had taken a vow of silence.

"How many men are at the Arches?" Roger demanded again, quietly.

Waldmann didn't answer.

"How many?" Roger insisted. "We don't want any bloodshed we can avoid.

We know exactly where they are. The place is surrounded, there isn't a chance of any of them getting out. How many are there? And what weapons have they got?"

Waldmann gulped; the muscles at his neck and his jaws worked, for a few moments it seemed as if he were going to be taken by a fit of shivering. There was a little clicking noise inside his mouth.

Roger took a packet of cigarettes from his pocket, shook some so that Waldmann could take one easily, and proffered the packet. Waldmann made no move to take one, although the fingers of his right hand were stained brown with nicotine.

"Waldmann," Roger went on, putting the cigarettes on the desk, "four of you are dead, two of you are under arrest. So that's six who will never benefit from the gold. But at least you and everyone caught alive will live. The law of the country says so." When Waldmann still did not answer, Roger continued in the same matter-of-fact voice: "The others haven't even the chance of escape that the Great Train Robbers had. They had a sporting chance, you and your friends haven't any chance at all. How many are there?"

Waldmann's neck and jaw muscles had stopped working, and defiance was back in his eyes, insolence crept back into his expression. Roger was sure, then, that the man would say nothing to help; that the police would have to make the raid blindly. Nothing under English law could break down Waldmann's silence. He could keep on trying but it would waste precious time.

He said: "All right, take him back to his cell."

Waldmann made no attempt to struggle, remained limp as the handcuffs were fastened again, turned sluggishly at first as if they were going to have to drag him out of the room. Then he turned on his heel, dragging against the cuffs, and spat into Roger's face. His own face blazed with hatred.

When the other men pulled him round and marched him off he didn't say a word; and now he made no pretence at dragging back. Roger felt a sense of hopelessness. As nearly sure as he could be that Flora Zigorski would not talk, he went into the washroom. As he dried himself on paper towels the telephone in the office rang, and he heard a man answer; almost on the instant the man appeared in the doorway, and spoke with obvious urgency.

"It's Commander Coppell himself, sir."

"I'll be there." Roger finished drying and tossed the towels into the waste bin, then went to the telephone. "Yes, sir?"

"Get anything out of Waldmann?" demanded Coppell.

"Absolutely nothing," Roger answered. "I'm going to see Flora Zigorski now."

"Well, don't be long," growled Coppell. "The Assistant Commissioner will sit in with us, and possibly someone from the Home Office. We've got to get those killers out of their hiding-place tonight, Handsome." After a pause, he added: "Whatever the cost, this has to be a show-down; the Yard's reputation depends on it. We want to do it ourselves, we don't want help from the Army."

Before Roger could reply, he rang off.

18

FLORA

ROGER put down the receiver, very conscious of the intense gaze of the policeman who had called him to the telephone. He dropped into a chair at the desk, and for the sake of saying something, asked:

"Is there a policewoman here, do you know?"

"Yes, sir — with the other prisoner."

"Ask the sergeant-in-charge to bring the woman prisoner in."

He was alone for a few moments, time enough to brood over Coppell's call. Its meaning was very simple, of course; no one at the top wanted a long-drawn-out siege, and there was something in Coppell's remark that the reputation of the Yard was at stake. That was too extreme, of course, but its reputation could be badly damaged if the Bullion Boys defied them long enough for an Army unit to be needed. He picked up the telephone and called

South West Division. The next moment he was speaking to the Map Inspector.

"Is there a detailed map and plan of the Arches?" he asked.

"Yes, Handsome."

"Send a copy over quickly, will you — this is going to be a showdown."

"You'll have it within half an hour," the Map Room Inspector promised. "Every possible way from those Arches is covered, you needn't have the slightest fear that they'll escape."

"Good," Roger said. "Thanks." In fact he wasn't at all reassured.

He had hardly put the receiver down before the door opened and Flora Zigorski was thrust inside by a policewoman. Two policemen came in immediately after them. There was no doubt at all that all of them were ruffled.

"The prisoner is being violent, sir," the policewoman reported, and held up her own and the other's hand. The expression on a long, thin, severe face was a plea for him not to have the handcuffs removed.

Roger sat without moving until the prisoner, glaring in a fury of defiance, was opposite him. Roger studied her with great deliberation; looking at her waist, the tight-fitting jeans, the tight-fitting jacket and a jumper which showed the gentle swell of her breasts. She was so young. He studied her neck and her chin, her mouth, concentrating for a few moments on every feature with a calculated manner which matched the insolence Waldmann had shown; and the tactics at least kept her quiet.

Then Roger stated almost casually: "You are remarkably like your father, Miss Zigorski. Especially at the eyes and forehead."

If he had struck her in the body, the effect could not have been greater. She actually seemed to sag, as if something which had held her stiff, had suddenly been pulled away. She put her free hand on the desk, as if to steady herself, and, like Waldmann's, her mouth dropped open. Her beautiful grey eyes became huge, the hardness in their expression changing to astonishment and alarm.

"We know everything, and we know that the rest of your group are at the Arches, in Hammersmith. Every way out of the Arches is sealed off." Then Roger said exactly what he had told Waldmann. "We don't want any bloodshed we can avoid. We know exactly where your accomplices are. The place being surrounded, there isn't a chance of any of them getting out. How many of them are there? And what weapons have they got?"

She began to breathe very heavily, her breast rising and falling. One of the policemen drew closer, as if expecting a new show of violence.

"Flora," Roger said in his most reasoning tone, "you could turn Queen's Evidence. It would make things much easier for you and you would almost certainly get a lighter sentence. You can't help the others to get away, the one good reason for silence doesn't exist any more. You can even help your friends — if we get them without a fight, they won't get hurt, won't suffer a lot of pain. There's no good reason for keeping silent, every reason to tell me all you can."

When he stopped, she grimaced, and for a moment he was afraid that it was with pain, it was characteristic of someone with severe stomach cramps. Had she taken poison? Could she have —

She burst out: "You fool. You bloody fool!" And then she exploded into such a torrent of foul-mouthed abuse, such obscenities, such gestures, that even Roger felt nauseated, and the policewoman looked shaken. Only the notetaker seemed unaffected, his ballpoint pen going smoothly on and on. Every now and again, between the obscenities and the blasphemies, she put in an intelligible phrase or two, and these registered vividly on Roger's mind: "They'll fool you. . . . You'll never catch them. . . . You're too late, a bloody sight too late." And then with a fury that seemed to shake every part of her body: *"Keep away if you want to live. . . . They'll blow you to pieces if you try to get in. . . . Keep away from the Arches."* And so she went on until at last Roger stood up, and said:

"Take her away." Ignoring the stream of oaths she hurled at him, he turned to the notetaker. "How long will it take you to transcribe the last part of her talk?"

"A matter of ten or fifteen minutes, sir."

"Bring the notes to my office, as soon as they're done." Roger ordered.

He saw Flora pulling against the handcuffs, suddenly; a writhing, heaving fury of woman, striking out, kicking at the groin of a policeman in front of her, a wild cat that two men and one woman found hard to control. When the room was empty Roger called for the Duty Sergeant. He was aware of nausea rather than disgust, recalling her father's agonised cry that the girl had been born with evil in her.

"How often has she been like that?" Roger asked when the man came in.

"Whenever anybody crosses her, sir."

"Has a doctor seen her?"

"Oh, yes, sir — Dr. Morgan. He's examining another prisoner now, sir, if you'd like a word with him."

"Please," Roger said. "Ask him to come here, will you?"

He leaned against the table when he was alone, thinking of the next half hour or so. There would be the report on the interview with Waldmann, the report on this interview, Venables' latest — every report that had been made. The Assistant Commissioner, Coppell, and whoever came from the Home Office could take their pick, but they would not be interested in detail, yet — only in how soon the raid was to take place.

Then Morgan, tall, thin, sallow-skinned, came in.

"I can guess what you want to know — has she been taking drugs?" he said before Roger had spoken. His voice had an unmistakable Welsh lilt. "I don't think so, Handsome, but I think she's demented. Yes, *mad*. Not in the conventional sense, perhaps, but psychopathic, subject to uncontrollable rages. I think you'll find she has a history of them."

Morgan went on and on...

"West," said Coppell into the telephone, ten minutes later, "when can you have the latest facts?"

"I have all I can get," Roger said.

"We shall meet in the Assistant Commissioner's office at six o'clock sharp."

That gave Roger five minutes.

He walked thoughtfully up a flight of stairs, trying to sort out in his mind everything that had been said, everything that needed emphasis. When he reached the Assistant Commissioner's door, it opened, and Coppell's secretary appeared, a little dowdy in a white blouse and a black skirt.

"They're all waiting," she said. "Lord Pentway has come from the Home Office."

Pentway was the Under-Secretary of State at the Home Office, second-in-command, and there could be no surer indication of the gravity of the view of the Home Office itself. He was a tall man, prematurely grey, for he looked in the early thirties. Anderson, the Assistant Commissioner, appointed only a short while ago and at the time expected only to last a few months, was proving much better than most. Coppell stood leaning against a corner of the square table.

"Ah, West," said Anderson. "Wish we hadn't to pressure you but we all feel there's no choice. You know Lord Pentaway, don't you? Good, good! Sit down." They all sat down, and Pentaway took out a pipe which was so encrusted round the edge of the bowl that it couldn't have been properly cleaned in ages. "What we need first is a brief assessment of the situation as you see it."

Roger pondered for a few moments before replying: "Extremely dangerous, sir. I've a feeling that both prisoners believe their accomplices will either get away with a lot of the gold, or do a great deal of damage before being caught." He placed a copy of the notes taken of Flora's tirade in front of each of them, and when they had finished reading he went on: "I think the woman is quite sure they'll get away, gentlemen. And I think they are nearly ready to go. They needed a little more time, that's why they tried to stop me from getting up to the Midlands. I'm sure they feared that I'd learn more about them through Zigorski."

"Are you implying that they've got something up their sleeve?" asked Lord Pentaway.

"The people at the Arches? Yes, I think they have, sir."

"And you've no idea at all what it is?"

"No," Roger admitted.

"You must have some idea, surely," Coppell said, exasperation in his tone.

"None," Roger said. "Except — "

The single word obviously affected the others. Pentaway paused in the act of lighting his pipe, then struck a match and pulled and puffed, eyeing Roger through the smoke. Coppell clenched his great fists and held them on the table. The Assistant Commissioner thrust his hands into his jacket pockets and then leaned dangerously back on his chair; it creaked.

"Except that they must have known, when they went there, that once they were suspected we could close all roads to and from the hiding place. And they must also have known that we could watch the railway track, and they couldn't get away along that. I've asked for a detailed plan of the Arches and one is on its way, but I know the area pretty well — I was involved in a case there a few years ago," he added. "I simply can't see these people hiding themselves in a place which could so easily become a trap."

"Do you mean you doubt whether they're there?" Lord Pentaway asked.

"Oh, they're there all right," answered Roger. "And they're sure they can get out."

"You mean they'll blast their way out," suggested Anderson.

"Any blast is bound to have repercussions," Roger said. "The whole area is too confined to take such a risk. No, they — "

The telephone nearest Coppell rang. Coppell glared as if resentful at the interruption, but picked it up. "Commander," he growled. "Who? . . . Can't I give him a message? . . . Oh, all right." He held the receiver out to Roger and said: "It's your man Green, West."

In the few seconds it took him to take the telephone and put it to his ear, Roger had time to prepare himself for a shock. Green, in normal circumstances, would have deferred on the instant to Coppell; for him to insist on talking to Roger meant he was under great stress. So it behove him to speak very calmly.

"Hallo, Sergeant," he said.

"*They're building a barricade across the approach to the Arches!*" Green burst out. "There's a big lorry on its side and some cement blocks and angle iron. They're getting ready to fight it out!"

The last words echoed from the earpiece about the room, and all three men with Roger heard it. Green's breath, very laboured, sounded as if he had been running.

"How many men have you seen?" Roger asked.

"At least four. They've blocked off about fifty yards altogether — the whole of the section at the far end, where it turns in a kind of L. You know what I mean, sir."

"Yes, I know," Roger said.

"And there's another thing, sir. No one from those end arches has gone home tonight. And also — " He broke off.

"Go on," Roger said.

"Excuse me, sir, here's Superintendent Wall," Green said. "He's been on the other line." There was a momentary pause before Wall came on. Only Coppell, of the three in the office, showed outward signs of impatience.

"Handsome," the other superintendent said, "I think we're in trouble."

"What kind of trouble?" Roger demanded, and saw Coppell lean forward.

"I've had a dozen reports including some from owners of businesses in the other arches near Number 27," said Wall. "They made one thing obvious: that

'To Let' notice was a dummy. The same people have had those end arches, the ones now barricaded off, for several years. They're all part of the Arches Tool & Machine Company. They employ between twenty and thirty men, and they specialise in high powered engines, motor racing and aero-engine parts. It's a small business and most of its sales are to European countries and to the Far East. They may have taken the gold to the Arches a few nights ago, but they didn't move in themselves as recently as that. They're always air-freighting spare parts to different countries in Europe, often by messenger. I've a list of names and addresses of the directors, but none of them seem familiar to me."

Roger said: "I'll come over, at once." He put the receiver down and repeated what he had just heard, adding briskly: "They might not have been aware of the danger of being trapped if they'd only just taken the premises, but they not only know they can be trapped, they're tightening the trap themselves."

"Are they *mad*?" asked Anderson.

"No, they're not mad, just sure of

themselves," asserted Roger. "And this is why they wanted to kill Angela Margerison so desperately. She knows the secret of the Arches. I wouldn't be surprised if Zigorski knows too."

"What the hell's the matter with you?" demanded Coppell. "What matters is — do *you* know?"

"There's only one thing it can possibly be, now," Roger stated flatly.

"Couldn't be more right," agreed the Assistant Commissioner roundly. "They mean to escape, they can't go by road or rail so there's only one way to go. By air, eh, West?"

"That's it, sir," Roger said. "That must be it. They've assembled one and possibly two helicopters. They've been smuggling the gold out of the country in small lots, hidden or somehow disguised as spare machine parts, and they're planning a getaway by air tonight. They're prepared for tear gas or C.S. gas to drive them out, and they feel completely secure, counting on surprise to get them and their pay load in the air before we realise what's going on."

"Do you propose to raid the Arches

before they leave?" enquired Pentaway.

"I think that would be crazy," Roger said. "Our only chance is to bring in the Army or Air Force. I should think that half a dozen helicopters wouldn't find it too difficult to force the escapers down over open country where they can do no damage." He was looking straight at Coppell, who was glowering. "Isn't that what you would recommend, sir?"

Before Coppell could reply, the Assistant Commissioner had picked up the telephone and was saying to the Under Secretary: "I take it you will confirm our need of help, sir. The Army is nearest, they can have helicopters here from Aldershot in less than half an hour." He glanced at Coppell. "Agree with you absolutely, Commander, it's the only thing to do."

Coppell's chest seemed to expand several inches as he drew in a deep breath, and then said in a growling voice:

"Oh, West had better have what he wants." He hoisted himself out of his chair. "Come on, West — it's time we were on our way to the Arches."

"There's one other possibility," Roger said. "They cleaned up Number 17, Lyon

Avenue but they haven't had time to clean up this place. They're bound to have had records, it's bound to be thick with giveaways. I would expect them to blow it up or destroy it by fire. Shouldn't we have a bomb disposal unit there, as well as fire fighting units?"

There was a long, tense silence, before Anderson said: "My God, you're right!"

"You are quite right, West," agreed Pentaway. "We will see to that. You go to the Arches."

Coppell led the way to the door.

19

THE ARCHES

ROGER sat next to Coppell in the back of the police car, the driver weaving his way through the late evening traffic. Another car with two more Yard officers and Venables was just behind. Roger nursed the radio; the line was open between the car and *Information*. Every now and again he peered up towards the sky, seeing red and green lights of aircraft or helicopters up there. He could not even guess if they were military.

"Mr. West." *Information* came clearly into the car.

"West here," Roger called back.

"Just heard that a helicopter *has* been pushed out of one of the Arches into the open space which is barricaded off."

Roger said: "How many men counted, so far?"

"Difficult to say with any accuracy, sir."

"Have we shown our hand?"

"No, sir. Division is standing by for instructions."

Coppell leaned forward.

"Commander Coppell here," he said gruffly. "Is there any news from the Army?"

"Six choppers on the way, sir. They're in constant touch with their command, and we have an open line to their command, too."

"Where are those choppers?" demanded Coppell.

"One moment, sir, and I'll find out."

The moment seemed to drag on interminably. They were in a bunch of vehicles including three buses which seemed huge and impassable, and a stream of traffic was coming towards them. The street lamps were misted, threatened by fog, and if fog fell quickly the Bullion Boys' helicopter could still get away. For these, in some ways the most tense moments of the affair, Roger sat helpless, not sure that he would be on the scene in time, if there should be trouble.

Information came back at last.

"Commander."

"Well, where are they?" demanded Coppell.

"Within sight of Hammersmith Bridge, sir, about to deploy. Mobile searchlights will pinpoint the Arches, sir."

Coppell grunted: "Right. Keep me informed."

"We will, sir."

The driver saw a gap between two buses, one going their way, one coming, and he thrust the nose of the car forward. There hardly seemed a coat of paint between them and the buses on either side, but they broke clear and a traffic-free stretch of road lay ahead; they were within sight of Hammersmith Broadway. The police motor-cycle patrols appeared, and sirens wailed. Soon, they were circling the big road junction with its five main roads. They were held to a crawl for a few moments and Roger craned his neck out of the window on one side, Coppell on the other. The traffic pulled in under orders from the motor-cycle patrols and the cars surged forward. The turn-off to the Arches was only two or three hundred yards away. In the distance a fire-engine bell clanged.

Suddenly, a dark shape appeared over the roofs of the houses, against the light of the stars. It had no lights but the glow above the streets and shops showed it clearly; and the growl of its engine came harsh and penetrating.

"My God!" gasped Coppell. "You were right."

The shape rose straight up into the air, and out of their sight. Traffic had been diverted so that the police cars ran into an open area. The driver pulled up, and switched off the engine. As it stopped the roar of another helicopter came and another dark shape appeared above the Arches themselves, also in darkness.

"*Two*," muttered Coppell.

"Probably the lot," Roger said.

"I hope to God the Army force them down."

"Can't be any serious doubt about that, sir," Roger soothed.

"All the same, I'll be damned glad when I hear."

"Calling Mr. Coppell and Mr. West!" *Information* broke in eagerly. "One helicopter has taken off from the Arches!"

"What's new?" growled Coppell.

"What was that, sir?" *Information* sounded startled.

"Forget it," Coppell said.

"We're at the Arches now," said Roger to the Yard. "Keep the line open all the time."

"*Anything going on?*" the *Information* man asked, almost pleadingly; and in spite of himself Roger laughed.

"Most of it up above," he said. "We don't know whether any of the Bullion Boys are left at the Arches. And we don't know what they've left there, either. Over."

Now, other policemen appeared from the road leading to the Arches, and two fire tenders pulled in, firemen in their steel helmets moving very fast. As Roger and Coppell hurried towards the barricade a Land-Rover turned into the cobbled approach road, and a youthful-looking captain climbed down from it. Roger heard the words:

"Bomb Disposal. Where's the explosive object?"

A policeman said: "There's Superintendent West, sir." Roger swung round. In the light of floodlights, headlamps and every lamp that could be turned on at the Arches, he looked very pale. Just ahead was the upturned lorry, great wheels upended, and at either side were heavy blocks of concrete and iron barriers. Obviously they had been welded together, wheeled here, and rammed beneath piles of cobbles prised up from the surface. Coppell was talking to the Divisional Superintendent, Green was standing by looking as if he couldn't wait to break into the conversation. Venables had appeared at Roger's side.

"Captain Hughes," the Bomb Disposal man announced.

"I'm West." They shook hands as Roger went on: "Have you been briefed?"

"Only that there's some trouble here. What is it? An old bomb or some landmines?"

Roger said: "The Bullion Boys were here until a few minutes ago. They've had to leave a lot of incriminating stuff behind, and we think they might have left delayed action bombs or incendiaries. You won't be able to use mine detectors, the place will be full of metal."

Captain Hughes was beckoning to his

unit, seven men in all. A sergeant appeared at his side.

"Sir."

"Sergeant, we have to make an exhaustive search of these Arches for H.E.s or incendiaries. Whatever they are I would guess they are small — like the one which caused the blow-up on the M1, Superintendent?"

"Could be." Roger marvelled at this man's matter-of-factness.

"Do you know how many Arches are involved?" Hughes wanted to know.

"No."

"Will some of your chaps volunteer?"

"I should be surprised if they won't," Roger said. "I will, for one."

"And me!" Venables put in, eagerly.

"If you'll get your men deployed, I'll get my instructions," Roger said, and he went forward to Coppell. The whole of the area beyond the lorry and the other barricades had been cleared in the middle, obviously for the helicopter take-off. One of the walls between two Arches had been taken down, and thus allowed ample room for the helicopters to be wheeled out. At the far end of these arches were massive machines — lathes and die-stampers, even part of a foundry; all of this was visible under the raking beam of a searchlight. Overhead a train roared, doubtless crowded with people who had not the slightest idea of what was going on.

"Commander Coppell — Captain Hughes. Captain Hughes would like some volunteers to help in the search, sir."

"Well, what are you waiting for?"

"Your approval," Roger said, and added: "We must have all train traffic over the Arches stopped, sir."

"Ought to have been done. I'll fix it," Coppell said.

"Excuse me!" Green stepped forward, a trumpet-like instrument in his hand. "I've a loud hailer, sir."

"Thanks."

Roger took it, placed it a few inches from his mouth and pressed the control button. He was aware of Coppell saying that Hughes was in charge of the search, of the local Superintendent saying that London Transport had already been warned to stop the trains and that if the Bullion Boys had left a time fuse they must have given themselves some grace in case there was a delay in take-off.

"Hallo, everybody," Roger called, and his voice sounded very loud, reverberating hollowly from the brick walls. "A bomb disposal unit is about to search the Arches for explosives and incendiary bombs which may have been left behind with delayed action fuses. Any man not doing a specific job can volunteer to help in the search."

"*Not the Fire Service,*" whispered Hughes.

"Not the Fire Service," Roger repeated.

Somebody near by said drily: "*They'll be needed to clear up the mess!*"

Someone else laughed.

Men began to move forward, plainclothes officers and uniformed men, until at least twenty were close by the overturned truck. They gathered round in a half-circle, with bomb disposal men among them. Hughes gave simple, precise instructions.

"Every apparent hiding place should be examined quickly, and any unidentifiable object should be drawn to the attention of my men. Since it takes time, space, and manpower — all, we presume, in short supply — to bury an explosive deeply or beneath heavy machinery, a number of small bombs, like hand grenades, seem most likely to be used. My men will go immediately to the office, since documents would probably be the first to be destroyed." He paused for a moment, and then called in a louder voice. "Ready? Let's go."

There was a strange hush, and stillness, before men began to file over the concrete blocks, climb over the lorry and down the other side. More lights were shone into the Arches. Roger let Hughes go ahead and took instructions from an Army sergeant.

"Second arch, sir, please. Follow me."

"Right."

Venables and Green followed in turn into a huge arched shed, the walls painted white, the floor with a thin covering of cement worn away in places. About the walls were pieces of heavy machinery, while everywhere was the heavy smell of oil. Piles of cast iron and of steel blocks were stacked tidily behind benches strewn with hand tools, vices, saws, and every kind of tool.

Roger approached one of the benches, Venables another, Green a third. Roger's heart was thumping, because the "bomb" he expected might be in the tool rack, in the drawer in front of the bench; anywhere. There was a sound of metal on metal as the search went on, a rustle of movement, a sound of breathing.

A man swore: and something crashed. The sound re-echoed and re-echoed and every man seemed to hold his breath.

"Sorry," one of the searchers muttered hoarsely.

"Mind my toes," complained another.

Roger finished his bench, Venables turned away from his, but Green was peering at something which lay on a nest of newspaper he had discovered under a tin can. He glanced round and called:

"Sergeant!"

The sergeant of the Unit came forward, looked at the object which was very like an egg, then lifted it slowly to his ear for what seemed an interminable time. He nodded.

"That's a little beauty," he said, and spoke over a loud-speaker attached to his jacket. "Captain Hughes, sir. One suspicious object found in Arch 29. It is made of aluminium, and is rather larger than a hen's egg and thinner. Halfway towards looking like a cigar wrapped in tinfoil, sir."

Almost immediately, Captain Hughes replied: "Everyone heard that description and now knows at least a type of suspicious object to look for. Bring it to me, Sergeant. The rest — carry on."

Less than two minutes later one of the Army men called out: "Another suspicious object here, sir, identical description with Sergeant Hall's."

As calmly as ever, Hughes called back: "Bring it here."

Another was found; a fourth, a fifth. Gradually a pattern emerged: the eggs were hidden beneath oily rags, wooden or steel shavings, beneath newspapers. Calls came announcing new finds minute after minute, and Captain Hughes made a kind of running commentary.

"That's Number 8, and we've just taken one of the little beauties apart. . . . It's incendiary with a pretty lively explosive charge to spread it about. . . . Most of the office and store rooms have been checked and rendered safe, as far as we can judge. . . . Number 10 coming up, and it does really begin to look as if incendiaries are all we have to worry about. . . . This little lot would have made an inferno of this place in about ten seconds from blast off. . . . We can't be sure but it looks as if the fuses were set for thirty minutes from the helicopters' take-off, say ten minutes from now. If there are any more of them about we'd better find them in a hurry."

Silence followed until a man knocked against some tin or light metal. After the clatter had died down came more silence; a fearful silence. Were there any other bombs or was Number 10 the last?

Venables whispered: "The ten minutes is up, surely?"

"He'll announce it," Roger said.

"Damn funny thing I found the first, wasn't it?" Green was delighted with himself.

"Yes," Roger said, and pulled some canvas gently off a pile that was probably steel or iron. Then, he stared at it. And Green and Venables gaped. Two men came over and joined them and one exclaimed: "My God!" Green said in a squeaky voice: "*Gold.*"

And it was gold; big bars of it, exactly as that taken from the ship and the lorry; a pile almost as high as Roger standing two feet from the wall; not half but at least a quarter of the stolen hoard.

But the rest was gone — some doubtless on those helicopters.

Had they been forced down?

Captain Hughes called: "We shall keep searching but it doesn't look as if we shall find any more booby traps tonight. I — "

There was a sudden, sharp explosion, and at the far end of his arch, a vivid burst of flame. A man called out; almost at once foam was being sprayed over the fire, new tension spread in case there were others, but Roger hardly gave that a thought as he studied the gold. He was still staring at it when Coppell arrived, eagerly.

"So now all we've got to do is find the rest," he remarked, but there was deep satisfaction in his voice. "Bloody good job of work, Handsome. And if you hadn't been so quick off the mark heaven alone knows how many men would have been killed."

Roger looked into that big, rather ugly face....

And just beyond it he seemed to see the face of Policewoman Nicholson. He couldn't bring her back, but at least he had made some amends. When he went out to see the crowds of newspaper, television and radio men, he was met by cheers which startled him. Near by both Venables and Green were grinning with delight, and Coppell was looking more pleased with life than Roger had ever seen him. There was deep relief among all the police, the firemen and the Disposal Unit men, a reaction from the time of danger. Then clearly above all the other sounds came a call.

"Superintendent West for *Information*, please. *Information* calling Superintendent West."

He moved towards the police car in which he had come here, took the telephone from the driver who was holding it at full stretch of its coil, and said. "West here."

"Those helicopters are down — both of them, sir. All the crew, sixteen men in all, are under arrest. They had a big cargo of gold on board, sir — a quarter of the total stolen, according to estimates."

Almost immediately afterwards a telephone message was passed on from the Rand Refineries. There was no doubt about the specimen being South African gold.

Very soon, one of the prisoners was talking freely, confirming the method they had used. The shop at the Arches had been the warehouse for the gold; here it was hidden, though too many people came in and out for it to be safe to do any work on it. Everything needed for the melting of the gold had been moved from the Arches, including some small cylinders of liquid propane gas, which produced a heat high enough to melt the gold. Domestic gas kept it molten, in the Krucibles, until it was poured into the test tubes, where it solidified. Had they been able to work for another month all of the gold bars would have been turned on the lathe, making shavings which were comparatively easy to melt down; and all of the ingots would have been distributed abroad.

Now most of the missing bullion was safe.

20
TENTACLES

CLEARING up was simply a matter of routine.

Search the small office at the Arches, get the names and addresses of the directors and the workers, all of whom were men, except for Flora Zigorski, on the records as Flora Smith, the only full-time office worker.

Meet the men who had been removed from the helicopters, identify, caution and charge them, then have each one searched.

Arrange visits, through the Divisions, to all the homes of the arrested men and the few who had not come in to work that day, and so had not been in the helicopters.

Learn that the leader of the thieves was a man whom Roger had seen once, a man who had received a seven-year sentence for robbery with violence and had been released only a year ago.

Learn that several of the others had records.

Learn that Margerison and the leader had quarrelled, Margerison challenging the leadership; learn that Margerison had left 17, Lyon Avenue not knowing he was soon to be murdered, having no thought of treachery. He had been followed by Waldmann and thrown into the Thames.

Learn that the other dead man, an engineer named Ross, had been on Margerison's side.

It was after three o'clock before Roger went home, an hour later than Coppell. Yard and Divisional men would work through the night and other shifts would take over from them, the pattern would be even clearer in the morning. There were notes from the boys: *Wonderful, Dad!* — Richard. *I don't know how you do it!* — Scoop. And there was a message from them both: *Mummy telephoned and sends her love, she says she watched a lot on television and is very proud of you. Let her know if you would like her to come back, if she doesn't hear she'll assume you'll be at the office till all hours.* He went up to bed, his mind buzzing with these messages, and with all he had learned and expected to learn tomorrow.

He did not set his alarm and it was after eleven when he did wake. At first he had assumed a telephone bell had disturbed him but if it had the call wasn't repeated. He called the Yard while still in bed, and the chief inspector who worked with him said:

"Everything ticking over perfectly, sir. The total amount of the gold recovered is well over half and we'll probably get a lot more yet."

"Good. Have you heard from the Commander?"

"He's not in yet, sir."

"Better! I'll be ready to leave in about an hour, and I'll go to the Arches first. Send a car for me, will you?"

"Yes, sir."

It was strange to be in the empty house, to get his own breakfast of boiled eggs and toast and ham, to have all the newspapers spread out, his photograph and that of the stacks of gold and of Captain Hughes on every front page. It was pleasant to scan the leading articles and to find the general tenor back to the old favourite: *The Yard Always Gets Its Man.* He was ready, shaved and dressed when a car drew up outside, and

Venables stepped out and came lolloping up the path. He was on the porch when Roger opened the door.

"Good-morning, sir!" Never had Venables' face been so bright.

"Good-morning," Roger said. "Can't you sleep?"

"Had a solid seven hours this morning, sir, and I happened to be in the inspector's office just after you telephoned. Seen the papers, sir?" he added eagerly.

"Yes. We're all heroes, aren't we?"

"Things simply had to go right," Venables remarked with his unbelievable naïvety. "They simply had to, sir!" They went out to the car and Roger was glad he had a driver. A crowd had gathered, newspapermen, photographers and reporters were still at the Arches in strength. Hughes was there, but about to leave.

"Everything's as clean as a whistle now, Superintendent."

"Would the place really have been burned out?"

"Enough stuff there to have started another fire of London," Hughes told him, and it was impossible to be sure whether he was serious or not.

Roger went straight to the Arches. Four Yard men were busy there, and Green was among them, looking bleary-eyed but happy.

"Good-morning, sir. We've made a lot of interesting discoveries this morning."

"Such as ?" Roger inquired.

"Well, sir, we found two small crates of machinery ready for shipment to the United States and one to Australia," stated Green. "Actually inside the spare motors for some electrical equipment there were some of the gold cigars." His eyes suddenly grew bright. "We ought to send someone to the different consignees to check and find the receiving agents, oughtn't we ?"

"We certainly should," Roger agreed.

Green must go to one country or the other; he deserved the break, Roger reflected. And Venables ? No, Venables could have his break with Appleby. Roger collected all the data available, including the names and addresses of over a hundred export customers, and went on to the Yard. It didn't surprise him that Coppell was in at last, and wanted to see him. He took the list along.

Coppell looked, for him, almost gracious.

"Couldn't have been a much cleaner job, Handsome," he applauded. "The Assistant Commissioner is very pleased; he has a luncheon appointment with Lord Pentaway tomorrow, and the Home Office will keep quiet for a while. Now — " He sat back in his chair and placed his great fists on the table. "How about *you*?"

Roger showed him the list of export customers, and showed photographs of the gold "cigar" hiding place in the two shipments found at the Arches.

"What we want is to have all these customers visited," Coppell decided. "Some will be in the clear but a lot may have gold stashed away. The local police will be only too glad to help, that's for sure. Any idea whom to send?"

"Yes," Roger said.

"Who?"

"Me," said Roger. "With Green."

Coppell looked startled, but suddenly gave one of his rare grins.

"Come to the conclusion that we can do without you here for a week or two, have you? Well, you're probably right. How long will it take you to clear up here, Handsome?"

"If I can delegate some of the work, I can be off in the morning," Roger told him. "The most likely customers seem to me to be those where shipments of spares have shot up in the past few months."

"South of France, California, South Africa and Australia, I presume," Coppell said, drily.

"I'd settle for Paris, New York, Johannesburg and Sydney," Roger replied, and when Coppell nodded his approval, he went on. "No objection if I take my wife along, is there? I'll pay for her, of course!"

Coppell pursed his lips.

"Don't see why not," he said. "But don't tell the world. If my wife gets to hear — " He broke off, and clenched his fists even more tightly. "I was to have gone to see our only daughter off to Canada, last night. Her husband's emigrating. My name is mud." He pushed himself away from the desk. I'll need a detailed report before you go, mind you."

"I'll see to it," Roger promised.

He felt a growing excitement as he went out, hardly able to believe that he would be able to make this round of visits. The excitement slackened only a little when he went to see Zigorski, who had stayed in a small hotel the previous night. While with him, Roger telephoned Crabb of K & K, and said quietly:

"I think Dr. Zigorski fears that his job is in jeopardy," Roger said.

"Well, it isn't," stated Crabb. "Tell him so, please . . . but don't tell him I'm glad that shrew of a daughter won't be round his neck any longer. He is quite the best research and maintenance man in our field, you know."

Roger told Zigorski about the job, and saw satisfaction slowly drive the dark shadows out of the old man's eyes.

Roger saw Angela Margerison, but she was still in a coma, and likely to be for some time. Fitzpatrick said over the telephone: "But she'll pull out of it, Handsome. She can't be more than twenty-two or three. She'll fall in love again, too — they never expect to, but people always do."

Roger put down the telephone, then called Green, who was still at the Arches. He would much rather take Venables, but rank alone made that unwise, and Venables would get plenty of breaks in future.

"Oh, Sergeant," he said. "I want a volunteer to come with me to the different customers overseas who might have received stolen gold in shipments already received. It could take a month altogether." He heard Green's stertorous breathing and realised the man didn't trust himself to speak. "Care to volunteer?" he asked.

"You — you actually *mean* it, sir?" Green almost squeaked.

"We need to start in the morning, for Paris," Roger said. "Finish what you're doing there, come and make your report up to date, and then go home and get packed." He rang off, and then pulled some reports towards him. They were Venables', all neatly typewritten and well-phrased; and the number of things he had noticed was quite remarkable. If he could overcome his squeamishness he would be a great asset to the Yard. Roger finished reading, and then sent for him.

"Venables," he said. "I'm going off with Sergeant Green to find the rest of the gold; we're bound to trace some of it, I think."

"Pretty well sure to," said Venables, without the slightest trace of disappointment. "I'd be grateful if I can stay on the case here, sir — the more I study it the more fascinating it becomes. If I — ah — but I'm sorry, sir, I'm speaking out of turn."

"What do you want to do?" asked Roger, fascinated.

"Ah — well, my shorthand's pretty good, sir, and if I could be present when senior officers are questioning the prisoners, and be in court this afternoon when they'll be charged and presumably remanded — "

Roger said: "There's an alternative, Venables."

"Is there, sir?" Venables covered up any sign of what he obviously expected to be a disappointment.

"Yes. Mr. Appleby has asked me for a man to be assigned to take notes for him during post mortem examinations," Roger said. "It's a rare opportunity, and one I had when I was fairly new with the C.I.D. You could find it very useful, and it could help you over the nausea problem."

Venables had turned very pale, and for a moment Roger felt that he had made a mistake, that the other would feel that he had to refuse. Well, it wasn't the end of the world, anyway.

Venables said very quietly: "If I ever make good in the Force, sir, I shall owe it to you. I'm *very* grateful, and of course I'll work closely with Dr. Appleby, too — it's a pretty trying time for him, sir. Did you know?"

"How trying?" Roger asked, as if he had no idea at all.

"He's going to be divorced, sir. It's in the *Globe* and several of the other papers this morning. Ah — again very many thanks, sir. It's a great privilege to work with you."

Roger waved his hands in a self-deprecating gesture.

Venables turned round very quickly and went out. The door closed quietly. Without him the room seemed very still and empty; a vacuum between two parts of the same case. Roger sat for some time and then pulled some files towards him and ran through the contents until he came across the photographs of Flora Zigorski, Angela Margerison and, finally, Rose Nicholson. He had hardly known Rose, and yet he seemed to have known her for a long time; and very well.

Soon, he put the photographs back in

their folders and put in a call to his wife, to tell her about the trip. He knew she would react with immediate delight, and have second thoughts about having to pack at such notice; and of course, she wouldn't have any clothes worth wearing!

Soon, he was saying: "I know, darling, but you can buy something in Paris, for a start, and..."

When at last he rang off, he felt very contented.

THE END

This book is published under the auspices of the
ULVERSCROFT FOUNDATION,
a registered charity, whose primary object is to assist those who experience difficulty in reading print of normal size.

In response to approaches from the medical world, the Foundation is also helping to purchase the latest, most sophisticated medical equipment desperately needed by major eye hospitals for the diagnosis and treatment of eye diseases.

If you would like to know more about the ULVERSCROFT FOUNDATION, and how you can help to further its work, please write for details to:

THE ULVERSCROFT FOUNDATION
The Green
Bradgate Road
Anstey
Leicestershire

We hope this Large Print edition gives you the pleasure and enjoyment we ourselves experienced in its publication.

There are now 1,000 titles available in this ULVERSCROFT Large Print Series. Ask to see a Selection at your nearest library.

The Publisher will be delighted to send you, free of charge, upon request a complete and up-to-date list of all titles available.

Ulverscroft Large Print Books Ltd.
The Green, Bradgate Road
Anstey, Leicester
England

J

FB
RS
PB
AS
KF
CJ

PB 11-9
AC
PM
4/01 PM